BEYOND THE
WHITE COAT

Dr. Atin Gupta

BLUEROSE PUBLISHERS
India | U.K.

Copyright © Dr. Atin Gupta 2024

All rights reserved by author. No part of this publication may be reproduced, stored in a retrieval system or transmitted in any form or by any means, electronic, mechanical, photocopying, recording or otherwise, without the prior permission of the author. Although every precaution has been taken to verify the accuracy of the information contained herein, the publisher assumes no responsibility for any errors or omissions. No liability is assumed for damages that may result from the use of information contained within.

BlueRose Publishers takes no responsibility for any damages, losses, or liabilities that may arise from the use or misuse of the information, products, or services provided in this publication.

For permissions requests or inquiries regarding this publication, please contact:

BLUEROSE PUBLISHERS
www.BlueRoseONE.com
info@bluerosepublishers.com
+91 8882 898 898
+4407342408967

ISBN: 978-93-6452-626-5

Cover Design: Dr Atin Gupta in association with SRL Creatives
Typesetting: Pooja Sharma

First Edition: August 2024

With humble hearts and spirits bright, We seek Lord Ganesha's guiding light.

Elephant-headed, with eyes so keen, Bestower of blessings, serene and seen.

In every page, His grace imbue, To write with purpose, firm and true.

Oh, Vighnaharta, hear our plea, Guide our words to set minds free.

With every line, let wisdom spring, In honor of Thee, our hearts shall sing.

> For this first book, our humble start, We offer Thee our deepest heart.

> May readers find in every part, Ganesha's grace, a work of art.

> So, bless our journey, sacred and pure, With Your presence, we are secure.

ACKNOWLEDGMENT

This book is the culmination of not just my thoughts and efforts, but the unwavering support, love, and encouragement from the people who mean the most to me. I would like to extend my deepest gratitude to my mother Late Smt Indu Gupta & my father Dr Pawan K Gupta whose wisdom and values have been my guiding light. Their belief in me, from the very beginning, instilled in me the confidence to pursue my dreams and aspirations.

To my beloved wife Dr Deepali Gupta, whose patience, understanding, and constant encouragement have been the bedrock of my journey. Your unwavering support has allowed me to dedicate the time and energy necessary to bring this book to life. You are my partner in every sense, and I am truly blessed to have you by my side.

To my wonderful children Anirudh, Kanav, Manit & Pavit, your joy, curiosity, and enthusiasm remind me daily of the importance of perseverance and hard work. You inspire me to strive for excellence in everything I do, and I hope this book serves as a testament to the power of dedication and commitment.

To my brother and sister-in-law Nitin & Ruchika, your constant motivation and support have been invaluable. Your belief in my work and your words of encouragement have fueled my determination to see this project through. I am grateful for your presence in my life and the positivity you bring.

Special thanks to Sh Subhash Garg & Sunita Garg for being my sounding board, my cheerleaders, and my source of strength. Your honest feedback, encouragement, and unwavering belief in my abilities have been instrumental throughout this process.

Finally, to my friends & everyone who has been a part of this journey, directly or indirectly, your positive influence has been crucial in the completion of this book. This work is as much yours as it is mine. Thank you from the bottom of my heart.

FOREWARD

Dear Readers

What it is to be a doctor.....

Why a doctor……

Let's hear a real world story

As Sakshi navigates the streets of her town in her memories, Sakshi recalls the pivotal moment that set her on the path to medicine. It was a crisp autumn day, leaves crunching beneath her small sneakers as Sakshi accompanied her ailing grandmother to the local clinic. Wide-eyed and curious, Sakshi witnessed the compassionate care provided by Dr. Atin, the town's beloved family physician.

The warmth of Dr. Atin's smile and the reassurance in his words left an indelible mark on young girl's heart. It was in that moment that the seeds of a calling were planted, and a dream took root. Inspired by the healing touch of Dr. Atin, Sakshi envisioned herself making a difference in people's lives, just like him.

The narrative unfolds with her journey through school, her unwavering determination and academic prowess set her apart. The challenges of rigorous coursework and the competitive nature of pre-medical studies fuelled her desire to excel. Encounters with inspiring mentors and captivating medical cases solidified her resolve, and Sakshi found herself on the doorsteps of medical school, ready to embark on a transformative chapter.

In the hallowed halls of the medical institution, Sakshi grappled with the complexities of anatomy, biochemistry, and the demanding schedule of a medical student. The highs and lows of her early years, the camaraderie forged with fellow students, and the unyielding passion that sustained her during the most challenging moments.

The readers are invited into her world as Sakshi discovers the multifaceted nature of the medical profession—its intellectual challenges, the emotional rollercoaster of patient interactions, and the first glimpses of the responsibility that comes with holding lives in her hands.

As the chapter unfolds her journey through medical school becomes a testament to resilience, dedication, and the unwavering pursuit of a lifelong calling. The foundations laid in small town blossom into a promising future, setting the stage for the impactful chapters that lie ahead in the Life of a Doctor.

BOOK INTRODUCTION

In the compelling pages of "Life of a Doctor," embark on a riveting journey through the highs and lows of a dedicated medical professional. This book delves into the heart and soul of the healing profession, exploring the intricate tapestry beyond the doctor's life.

From the moment the calling is discovered to the culmination of a fulfilling career, each chapter unravels a different facet of the medical world. Readers will witness the transformative years of medical school, the intense and demanding experience of residency, and the adrenaline-fueled moments in the emergency room.

As our protagonist advances, the book delves into the delicate balancing act between professional commitments and personal life. Through the eyes of a seasoned doctor, witness the triumphs and the heart-wrenching losses, the moments of medical marvels, and the challenges faced in the pursuit of specialization.

The narrative broadens its scope as the doctor embarks on global health adventures, showcasing the impact of healthcare beyond borders. In the operating room, experience the precision and pressure of life-saving procedures, and outside, discover the significance of mentoring the next generation of healers.

The book takes a thought-provoking turn, exploring the changing landscape of healthcare and the silent struggle of burnout. As the doctor grapples with medical ethics, readers are invited to reflect on the moral compass that guides these professionals through challenging decisions.

In the final chapters, the book paints a portrait of a doctor's legacy beyond the white coat. Through reflections on a fulfilling career, the narrative comes full circle, leaving readers with a profound understanding of the Life of a Doctor and beyond………..

This BOOK is for anyone interested in learning more about the daily life of a doctor, from medical students to aspiring healthcare professionals. It's an inside look at both the challenges and rewards of this career path.

CONTENTS

A DAY IN THE LIFE OF A DOCTOR: MY PASSION 1

THE PURSUIT OF HAPPINESS IN MEDICINE 10

NAVIGATING THROUGH SADNESS 21

TRIUMPHS & TRIALS IN THE ER 32

UNDERSTANDING FINANCIAL ASPECTS OF BEING A DOCTOR 43

COMMITMENTS TO CONTINUING MEDICAL EDUCATION 51

BALANCING PROFESSIONAL AND PERSONAL LIFE: KEY INSIGHTS 61

MANAGING STRESS AND PRESSURE IN MEDICAL PRACTICE 72

BUILDING RELATIONSHIPS: PATIENT INTERACTIONS 81

THE IMPORTANCE OF TEAMWORK IN HEALTHCARE 92

EXPLORING SPIRITUALITY IN THE MEDICAL FIELD 101

LEGACY BEYOND THE WHITE COAT 112

FINAL THOUGHTS 122

1

A DAY IN THE LIFE OF A DOCTOR: MY PASSION

Before we delve into different aspects of "The Life of a Doctor", I wanted to give you an inside look into a day in my life as a doctor. I hope this grabs your attention as I share my journey and passion for medicine.

From the moment I wake up, my mind is focused on helping others.

As a resident doctor, the challenges start early. The alarm goes off at 5 a.m., assuming I'm lucky enough to get any sleep at all. After rushing to get ready, off to the hospital to begin a 12+ hour shift. The mornings are consumed with a seemingly endless string of patient visits, each presenting their own set of complex health issues that require diagnosis and treatment.

The job only gets more demanding as the day wears on. The endless charting, dictations, and paperwork pile up, stealing time away from actual patient care. Lunch breaks are rare. Bathroom breaks are a luxury. The constant needs of patients mean a doctor is always on call, even if they manage to wolf down a snack to keep their energy up.

By the time the shift finally ends, exhaustion has already set in, but the day isn't over. There are still notes to complete, prescriptions to write, and labs to follow up on. The sacrifice of a personal life is par for the course, knowing that in a few short hours, the whole chaotic routine starts over again.

As a consultant, I start my day with morning rounds. As I walk from room to room, I'm filled with enthusiasm and care for each of my patients. Hearing their stories and learning about their lives gives me empathy and motivates me to provide the best care possible. The life of a doctor is demanding but rewarding. It requires years of education and training, long work hours, and immense dedication. But doctors get to make a real difference in people's lives every day.

Ever wondered what it's like to be a doctor? From gruelling years in med school to marathon shifts in the ER, a doctor's life is not for the faint of heart. But it's also deeply meaningful work that impacts lives daily. On the one hand, they get to make a huge difference in people's lives by diagnosing illnesses, performing surgeries, and prescribing treatments. But it comes at a cost — gruelling shifts, enormous stress, and difficult choices.

Despite the difficulties, most doctors find the work incredibly meaningful. There's no greater feeling than helping patients heal and recover. And while the job is stressful, doctors take pride in developing expertise and making the right calls under pressure.

Rounds are followed by scheduled surgeries, appointments, and meetings. The variety keeps me engaged and allows me to apply years of medical knowledge. Whether I'm performing a complex surgery or having a thoughtful discussion with a patient, I feel immense satisfaction being able to make a difference in someone's life. At the end of the day, I know I've impacted lives in a positive way. If you have the brains, work ethic, and emotional intelligence to handle the demands of the job, a career in medicine can be hugely satisfying.

While being a doctor requires long hours and constant learning, I wouldn't trade it for anything. The opportunity to diagnose, treat, and interact with patients on a daily basis is an honor and privilege. I'm filled with desire and passion to keep growing in this meaningful career.

Dr. Sakshi still remembers the moment she decided to become a doctor. At ten years old, she was hospitalized with pneumonia. The compassionate gesture of Dr Atin, who treated Sakshi, made her feel calm and cared for during a scary time. From that point on, she knew she wanted to provide that same comfort to patients. After finishing her residency, Dr. Sakshi now works in the paediatric ICU. Though shifts are long and work is demanding, she finds joy in comforting scared children and providing excellent care. The hardest moments make the rewarding ones shine even brighter.

The long road to becoming a doctor and the day-to-day challenges are all worth it to positively impact people's lives during vulnerable moments.

The life of a doctor is often glamorized in TV shows and movies. We see the dramatic emergencies, the fascinating procedures, and the prestige that comes with the white coat. But what we don't see is the years of intense study and training it takes to become a doctor. The long days and sleepless nights spent poring over dense medical textbooks and flashcards. The gruelling hours in the hospital on-call, being woken up at all hours of the night to deal with new admissions and emergencies. We also don't see the emotional toll this career can take — having to deliver bad news to patients and families or losing a patient on the operating table. The reality is that being a doctor requires an immense amount of dedication, perseverance, and sacrifice.

After completing four years of medical school followed by one year of Internship and then three years of residency, doctors are finally specialized and licensed to practice medicine. At this point, the rewards start to come. There's the satisfaction of making the correct diagnosis and choosing the right treatment to save a patient's life. There's the thrill of performing a high-stakes surgery or procedure successfully. And there's the joy that comes with developing long-term relationships with patients and walking with them through their healthcare journey. Of course, challenges remain. Doctors must keep up with new advancements in their field through continuing education. They often have hectic schedules balancing clinic and hospital duties. And there's always the risk of burnout from such a demanding profession. But overall, the life of a doctor is one of service, mastery, and profound purpose that nobody can match.

The journey to becoming a doctor is arduous, but also deeply meaningful. It takes a special kind of perseverance and commitment to complete the rigorous training. But for those who can endure, a life of service, expertise and fulfilment awaits on the other side. Doctors are the heroes who keep our communities healthy. Their journeys are filled with inspiration, passion, and purpose.

When I think about my childhood best friend Rohit who recently became a doctor, it reminds me of the great sacrifices doctors make to follow their calling.

Rohit dreamed of being a doctor since high school after volunteering at the children's hospital. He worked tirelessly through medical school, pulling all-nighters studying complex diseases and treatments. During his residency, ROHIT survived on little sleep, working 36-hour shifts in the ER saving lives.

Did you know that doctors work an average of over 50 hours per week? That's more than most other professions! As professionals and aspiring leaders, we can relate to the grind of long work weeks. But for doctors, this intense schedule is their normal.

Whether you're a doctor yourself or know one personally, you understand the demands of this career. The endless days of seeing patients, managing staff, and keeping up with new research and treatments take a toll. Despite the challenges, most doctors wouldn't trade it for anything. They find purpose in healing others.

Now as an attending physician, the life of a doctor is still filled with sacrifice. I often miss family events and holidays because someone's life depends on me being at the hospital. Yet I loves being able to make a difference for my patients. My purpose makes the sacrifices worthwhile.

I still remember the day when I went to a marriage with my family. The food was not served yet, and I received an emergency call from the hospital. I had to rush without wasting any time and was not able to inform my family because some other family members were waiting for me. I reached the hospital on time to finally save the patient. Meanwhile, my family had to come back home taking a lift. That day my family decided that we should go separately while attending social gatherings, a hilarious moment.

Doctors are everyday heroes. Their journeys require great commitment, sleepless nights, and missing life's special moments. But they find deep fulfilment in improving lives and serving humanity.

Next time you see a doctor, remember the incredible journey they embarked on to follow their dreams. Their passion and sacrifices make our communities healthier and stronger. We're lucky these everyday heroes are willing to give so much of them to care for us.

So the next time you're tempted to complain about working late, remember the doctor who is just starting their shift. Let's have gratitude for the passion that drives them. And if you're a doctor reading this — thank you. Keep fighting the good fight. Your dedication makes a difference.

If you also have a heart for helping others, I encourage you to explore the medical field. With hard work and dedication, you too can find purpose in improving lives.

Have any of you considered a career in medicine? What appeals to you about this demanding but meaningful profession? Have you ever wondered what it's like to be a doctor? The long hours, high stakes decisions, and emotional rollercoaster that comes with saving lives. It's a career path like no other. The next generation of doctors will continue the noble tradition of healing and saving lives. It's a calling for those willing and able to answer it.

I'd love to hear your thoughts! Feel free to connect with me if you'd like to learn more about my journey. I'm happy to provide guidance and advice.

Remember the long road they travelled to attain that white coat and stethoscope. Let it inspire us to respect and show gratitude for the profession. So, if you visit your doctor and see just how tired they look, remember the immense burden they carry for the sake of others. Offer those thanks and understanding, rather than complaints. And know that despite the trials, their efforts are truly making a difference in this world **—one patient at a time please…….**

Wishing you all the best in pursuing your passions.

My contact details: <u>authordratin@gmail.com</u> or WhatsApp me @ 9888079179

2

THE PURSUIT OF HAPPINESS IN MEDICINE

The Never-ending Joy of Being a Doctor

This is for all the doctors, nurses, and healthcare professionals out there experiencing the emotional rollercoaster of caring for others. Let's take a moment to appreciate the happy glimpses that make it worthwhile.

Only 46% of physicians say they feel happy and fulfilled in their career. Yet despite the stress, there are still many rewarding moments.

That's why it's so important to cherish the happy moments that make everything worthwhile. Those special moments that remind us of the privilege it is to care for others. Here are some of the happiest times in a doctor's life.

How Doctors Find Meaning and Happiness in Their Work

Do you ever wonder what makes doctors happy? To find meaning in taking care of one's health. Life as a doctor can be incredibly rewarding, It's important to cherish the happy moments.

As a doctor, the happiest moments are when you get to save a life or improve someone's health. There's no greater feeling than knowing you made a difference for a patient.

From the first time you detect an illness and make an accurate diagnosis, to seeing a patient recover after a successful surgery you performed, it's a series of memorable moments. Even just having a patient thank you for your care means the world. Their trust in you is an honor.

From delivering babies to curing illnesses, doctors get to experience profound joys. Though the job comes with challenges, there are many bright spots that make it all worthwhile.

While dealing with life-and-death situations is never easy, doctors take pride in using their skills to heal others. The human connections they build are incredibly comforting. Seeing a patient recover or a disease caught early brings a profound sense of accomplishment. As a doctor, you'll experience incredible highs that make all the hard work worthwhile. There's nothing quite like the feeling of getting to be there for people during their times of greatest need. It's a special privilege.

For those drawn to medicine, the chance to make a difference outweighs the challenges. There's something special about being trusted with people's lives. It's a humbling privilege and honor.

Unforgettable Moments

I'll never forget the first time I delivered a healthy baby during internship, I had cared for the anxious parents all through a high-risk pregnancy. After hours of labor, the mother's face lit up when she held her new born. It was magical to welcome this precious life into the world. The tears in their eyes as they held their precious new born is something I'll never forget. Hearing that first cry as the parents beamed with joy brought tears to my eyes. It made years of my hard work worthwhile.

Another standout moment was when I diagnosed a rare condition in a young patient that others had missed. The look of relief on her face when I provided an answer for her symptoms was incredibly fulfilling. The patient I had treated for years hugged me — his cancer was finally in remission. The time I spotted a cancerous tumour early and was able to remove it before it spread. Sharing the good news with a terrified patient that we caught it in time is a rush like no other. These are the moments I live for. I could see the relief and joy on her face. It was incredibly humbling and uplifting.

And then there are the children who run up to give me a hug and a drawing when they see me in the hospital. Their innocent smiles and unconditional trust are like a soothing balm for the soul.

A Heartfelt Gratitude

In Indrani Hospital, we receive an abundance of blessings while caring for the elderly.

Kuldeep kaur, 72, expressed heartfelt gratitude to each and every one of us for the exceptional care and treatment she received. She continued, saying that the dedication, professionalism, and kindness possessed by team of Indrani Hospital made a significant difference in my recovery journey. Further saying that she felt truly blessed to have been under our care.

She added "May you continue to touch the lives of many others with your compassionate care and may you be blessed abundantly for the incredible work you do. God bless you Dr. Atin".

My another patient Mrs. Susham Bala mother of Mr. Praveen, shared golden words which brought tear to my eyes "Doctor sahib, bache maa ki vajah se hote hain par hamari maa aap ki vajah se hai"

Mrs. Santosh Sidhu was so much impressed about the passionate care she received from our hospital that she gifted a wheel chair on her 70th birthday to our hospital.

Touching Incident

Just before the start of Ganesh Chaturthi in 2023. I was referred to a very poor patient by a friend, offered to pay for her expenses. The patient was severely anaemic with complains of breathlessness. Despite the financial burden, we admitted her and provided with blood transfusion. While informing about me the relative expenses, something transpired quite differently. As soon as we started her treatment, a hint of smile from the patient graced my heart. After the discharge, I discovered she made sculptures for a living. Touched by her story, I waived her charges. Fifteen days later, she brought me a handmade sculpture of Ganapati Idol, which I now keep in my OPD room as a symbol of purest blessings.

दैनिक भास्कर   बठिंडा भास्कर   19-09-2023

गणपति की मूर्ति बनाने वाली महिला का मुफ्त में किया इलाज

बठिंडा | इंद्राणी हॉस्पिटल में मूर्ति बनाने वाली एक गरीब महिला का इलाज मुफ्त में किया गया। जिससे पूरी तरह ठीक होने की खुशी में उसने अपने हाथों से बना कर और रंग कर के श्री गणपति की भव्य मूर्ति डॉक्टर अतिन गुप्ता को भेंट करी। इंद्राणी हॉस्पिटल के एमडी डॉ. तिन के अनुसार इस गणेश चतुर्थी इससे बेहतर तोहफा शायद और कुछ नहीं हो सकता। उन्होंने कहा कि हमें निस्वार्थ अच्छा काम करते रहना चाहिए क्योंकि हमारे कर्म ही घूमकर हमारे पास वापस आते हैं।

Of course, there are the countless thank you cards and baked goods that patients bring to show their gratitude. Those mean so much, knowing I made a difference in their lives.

And the story continues…………..

Yes, being a doctor has its challenges. But it also has rewards beyond measure. Those special moments when you know you've made a real difference in someone's life – that's what makes it all worthwhile. The emotions I've felt at patients' happiest moments are indescribable. I'm grateful to play a role, however small, in these joyful life events.. The ability to profoundly impact people's lives for the better is an honor and privilege. I'm thankful every day that I get to experience such joy in my work.

The Emotional Bonds

As doctors, we experience a wide range of emotions. The highs and lows are all part of the job. However, the moments that really make it meaningful are when we get to make a positive impact on a patient's life. Whether it's diagnosing an illness early, witnessing a successful surgery, or simply putting a smile on a sick child's face — these are the memories we strive for. The relationships we build with patients and their families are incredibly rewarding. When a patient trusts you with their life, it's a humbling and empowering feeling. Being there during major life events like childbirth or end-of-life care creates a bond that goes beyond medicine. We become healers, counsellors and supporters for those needing it most.

So next time you're feeling bogged down, remember those happy moments. Cherish the hugs, the tears of joy, and the smiling faces. Let them re-energize your spirit and remind you why you chose this noble calling.

Because no other job allows you to combine intellectual rigor with genuine care and compassion. Focus on developing empathy, resilience and a passion for service. With the right mind-set, a career in medicine can be incredibly meaningful and filled with small, happy moments every single day.

Finding Happiness

Though being a doctor is difficult, the happy moments – big and small – make it incredibly fulfilling. Focusing on these keeps me going on the hard days.

If you want a career that allows you to do meaningful work, consider healthcare. With empathy, dedication and compassion, you too can find daily happiness helping others. While the road is long, the destination is worth it.

As young professionals starting your careers, you know the trials of student debt. Imagine finally paying off those loans and becoming financially stable.

For doctors, that moment comes after nearly a decade of training. Finally becoming an attending physician and earning a real pay check is incredibly liberating. No more counting pennies: you can finally buy a house, start a family, and take a well-deserved vacation. Financial freedom is a major milestone.

But the real happy moments come from the patients. When a surgery goes flawlessly and you see that patient recovering happily, it makes all the hard work worthwhile. Or when a terminal patient thanks you wholeheartedly for the extra time you spent with them. Those human connections make a lasting impact.

In the end, despite the stress, most doctors are grateful to be able to help people. Now, years into my career as a doctor and successfully running Indrani Multi specialty Hospital, I can't imagine doing anything else. Feeling of being a young entrepreneur, successfully running a multispecialty hospital, taking care of critically sick patients, providing dialysis facility and managing a blood bank by motivating people for blood donations and saving lives along with doing social activities like free treatment in slum areas are all that things brings satisfaction and happiness.

Real-time Achievements

The appreciation I have received from Mr. Rahul IAS, Commissioner MCB (left) for my contribution in Swatch Bharat Abhiyan, award at BNI for best performing Director Consultant (centre), and appreciation award from DC Mr. Arvind Pal Singh Sandhu for extra ordinary contribution during COVID times(right).

For those considering a career in medicine, know that it's not easy. You'll have many long, exhausting days. But you'll also have days that remind you why you chose this path. Days when you connect with patients, ease their fears, and make a real difference. In the end, a career in medicine is defined by the happy moments - the times you positively impact another life. Cherish those moments. They're what make everything worth it. ,What are some standout happy moments you've experienced in your career? I'd love to hear your stories.

Write down to me what you feel @ My contact details: authordratin@gmail.com or Whatsapp me @ 9888079179

And my dear patients next time you visit your doctor, know that they cherish the opportunity to help you. Those moments of healing are the happy highlights of our days.

BEST MOMENTS IN A DOCTOR'S LIFE.

- Cry of a new born

- Waking up of a comatose patient

- The sound of restarting heartbeats when resuscitating a patient

- The genuine Thank You of a patient relieved of pain / stress / illness

- When someone randomly recognizes you in public and thanks you in front of your kids / family

- When the poorest of the poor collect enough money and gift you sweets for treating them free

- When anyone at work says Take some rest now. You have been working too much

- When someone says I want to become a Doctor like you

3

NAVIGATING THROUGH SADNESS

In the stillness of the hospital corridors, where the beeping of machines echoes like a haunting melody, there lies a tale of heart-wrenching despair. It's a story that unfolds too often in the sterile confines of the ICU, where life hangs by the thinnest thread, and hope dances on the edge of a scalpel.

As doctors, we experience the full spectrum of human emotions. While there are plenty of joyful moments caring for patients, there is also difficult, heart breaking ones. This chapter reflects on some of the saddest parts of being a physician.

Most people see doctors as miracle workers who save lives. But behind their white coats, stethoscopes, and confident smiles, doctors experience profound sadness and grief. Despite the prestige and financial rewards, a doctor's life is filled with difficult moments. Long hours, immense pressure, and emotional turmoil often lead to burnout, depression, and cynicism.

With the right self-care, doctors can have long, fulfilling careers. We must have realistic expectations, knowing we will inevitably encounter profound sadness. This is the price of compassion.

Saving lives, helping people, using your skills and knowledge to make a difference — it's a noble profession. But behind their confident white coats are human beings carrying heavy emotional burdens. With each loss or trauma, doctors grieve in their own quiet ways while continuing to care for others. Their pain and grief are an unseen side of medicine.

In medical school, we're taught to "never get too attached" to patients. But in reality, caring deeply about our patients is precisely what makes us good doctors. And with that care comes heartache when things don't go as hoped.

One of the hardest things a doctor must face is losing a patient. Despite your best efforts, sometimes you cannot save a life. Nothing prepares you for the gut-wrenching feeling of telling a family their loved one is no more. The weight of the failure sticks with you.

A Heart-Wrenching Incident

The patient was a 28-year-old female, diagnosed with stage 4 breast cancers. Over the next two years, we celebrated milestones like finishing chemo and getting engaged, but the cancer kept returning. When I got the call that hospice had been consulted, I excused myself to cry in a supply closet. Losing a patient — especially one so young — never gets easier. As their doctor, you form a bond and get to know them on a personal level. When their health declines and eventually pass away, it feels like losing a friend.

Grief is an inevitable part of practicing medicine. But it's also what connects us to our shared humanity. The privilege of being with people during their most vulnerable moments is worth the pain that comes with it.

Another sad moment is delivering a severe diagnosis. Having to tell someone they have cancer or a terminal illness is devastating. You wish you could take their pain away. It's emotionally draining to shatter someone's world with bad news, even when delivered with empathy.

Doctors also witness tremendous suffering. Terminally ill patients in agonizing pain. Children with incurable diseases. Victims of violence and accidents. It takes a huge emotional toll to confront such trauma daily.

Watching patients suffer is also agonizing. Despite your best efforts, sometimes you can't ease their pain or improve their condition. The helplessness and frustration take an emotional toll. You go into medicine to heal people, so it's hard to accept the limits of what you can do.

What if you were the one holding a life in your hands?

Being a doctor is a unique profession that comes with immense responsibility. You are entrusted with people's health and lives. The decisions you make can have profound impacts.

Doctors go through intense training to prepare for this immense duty. Yet nothing fully prepares you for the difficult moments. When a life hangs in the balance, and the outcome is uncertain. When you have to deliver heart breaking news to a patient or their family. When you, despite your best efforts, lose a patient.

I'll never forget the first time I lost a patient under my care. She was a young mother of two, in septic shock. Over the time, I had gotten to know her and her family and was determined to save her. On a cold Tuesday morning, I got the call that she had passed away. As I absorbed the news, the weight of failure fell heavy on my shoulders. I second guessed my decisions, wondered what more I could have done. Later, speaking with her husband and the pain in his eyes, my heart broke.

Another incident was during COVID times. Nobody was prepared, nobody was taught in their medical schools, it was an emergency for which doctors, nursing staff, NGO's, ambulances were on front foo. Even primary relatives of the patient did not take them to the hospital.

At that time, Indrani Hospital was the first one to provide COVID services in our city, Bathinda. We had a huge success rate of recovery, until we lost a young male patient. While death was common during COVID times, this was particularly tragic because he left behind his wife and two small daughters. What brings solace is his wife and kids remain connected with us, appreciating the care and efforts we made to save his life.

Being a doctor requires resilience to get back after difficult moments. What sustain us are the lives we do save, the illnesses we cure, and the patients we help. We have the profound privilege of making a difference. Though the path is often trying, it remains deeply rewarding.

To withstand the rigors of the job, doctors need coping strategies. Connecting with colleagues helps, as they understand the unique stresses you face. Setting boundaries and taking time off keeps you refreshed. Developing outside interests and relationships provides balance. And accepting limitations — medicine cannot save everyone — helps make peace with loss.

This stress makes me remember of one of my classmate who, at one point of time couldn't share his feelings and was left alone — good by heart, gem of a person, a helping hand was lost.

The usual bustling activity is subdued, replaced by hushed whispers and anxious glances. For in one of the pristine rooms, a college friend, a comrade in the journey of youth and dreams, battles against the merciless grip of mortality.

While there are heavy emotional burdens, the privilege of caring for others also makes being a doctor meaningful. The sorrowful moments remind us of the humanity in medicine. By supporting each other through the ups and downs, doctors can find purpose and resilience. The heartbreak inspires us to connect more deeply with patients, improve care, and make the most of every day.

While everyone experiences grief, perhaps no profession understands its depths like doctors. We grieve for patients, their families, and the lives cut short by disease. Every beep of the monitor feels like a hammer blow to the chest, a reminder of the fragility of existence. Each passing moment is a cruel reminder of how swiftly life can slip away, leaving behind a chasm of grief and regret.

In the ICU, time seems to stand still, frozen in a perpetual state of agony. The doctors and nurses move with a sense of urgency, their faces etched with determination, yet tinged with resignation. They fight tirelessly, wielding their expertise like a shield against the relentless march of fate.

But amidst the flurry of medical interventions and whispered prayers, there is a sense of helplessness that hangs heavy in the air. Despite the advanced facilities and cutting-edge technology at our disposal, there are battles that even the most skilled healers cannot win.

The life of a doctor is filled with highs and lows. There was heart breaking moments that leave an indelible mark. As a doctor, I've witnessed my share of tragic cases that still haunt me.

I remember a 7-year-old boy battling leukaemia. Despite multiple rounds of chemo, the cancer kept spreading. As his tiny body slowly shut down, his parents wept inconsolably. We did everything medically possible, but it wasn't enough. Losing a patient so young is always devastating.

Another incident etched in my mind is a fatal car accident involving a newlywed couple on their honeymoon. The husband died on the spot while the wife survived but slipped into a coma. Seeing her family keeping vigil by her hospital bed for weeks, praying for a miracle that never happened, was gut-wrenching.

As a critical care expert, I've seen staggering trauma cases – victims of shootings, stabbings and assaults. Trying desperately to save them knowing their lives hang by a thread takes an emotional toll. Informing families that their loved one didn't make it is the hardest part of my job.

Being a doctor brings fulfilment but also sorrowful, haunting moments. Losing a patient — whether a child, a young person in their prime or the elderly — never gets easier. But it's remembering their faces and stories that drives me to save the next life. The heartbreaks remind me of the fragility and preciousness of life.

And so, as I stand outside that sterile room, my heart heavy with sorrow. In the face of such profound loss, words fail me, and all I can do is offer a silent prayer, as they embark on their final journey beyond the confines of this world.

But still we keep going because of the good we can do.

According to a 2017 survey, over 40% of doctors report feeling burned out.

As professionals, many of us have demanding jobs that require long hours and take a toll on our mental health. This is especially true for those in the medical field. Dealing with life and death on a daily basis can lead to grief, stress, and compassion fatigue. Watching patients suffer, making mistakes, or losing a patient are sad realities doctors face.

Doctors lead challenging lives. Beyond long work hours and high stress, they regularly face profound sadness. From losing patients to breaking difficult news to families, a doctor's job brings frequent sorrow.

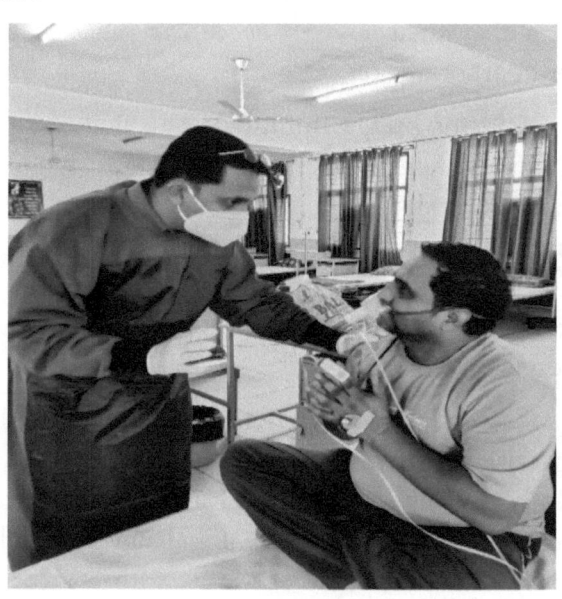

Doctors deserve more understanding and support. Their sadness and distress are valid, though hidden, and their mental health impacts their ability to care for us. We must recognize the humanity and vulnerability behind the stethoscope. Simple gestures like asking "How are you?" and truly listening can make a difference.

I still remember when a patient called Divya came to see me. Before I could inquire about her problem, she started with ' *hello doctor, how are you?'* I just replied that I am fine and thanked her. For a moment, I felt relaxed, knowing that someone cared about my well-being. People often see us as superhuman, who can't get sick, but Divya's simple question reminded me that I was human.

Dear readers, reach out to the doctors in your life. Ask how they're coping and feeling. Watch for signs of burnout, and encourage them to prioritize self-care. Remind them they don't have to carry their burdens alone, share stories of doctors' grief to build empathy. Advocate for improved mental health support in medicine. Their mental health and wellbeing enables them to provide the best possible care. Appreciate the whole person behind the physician – their griefs along with their gifts. Together, you can ease the unspoken sadness in a doctor's life.

Despite the challenges, most doctors find deep meaning in their work. The ability to alleviate suffering and walk with people during vulnerable times is a privilege. With experience, doctors learn healthy ways to process the difficulties and continue finding purpose in their calling.

In between the triumphs and fulfilment are heart-wrenching moments. It takes resilience to not become hardened. The key is having support systems, perspective and remembering the times you made a positive impact. Every doctor has stories of devastating cases, but they also have stories of hope. Focusing on those moments of healing, breakthrough and gratitude helps they continue their mission. It's an honor to care for people in their darkest hours. By building compassionate communities around themselves, doctors can share the heavy burden and keep their hearts open.

Have you ever felt grief in your work? How did you cope with profound loss on the job? I'd love to hear your stories and insights.

This is for all the healthcare professionals out there who have experienced grief at work. Your feelings are valid, and you're not alone.

Write down to me what you feel @ My contact details: authordratin@gmail.com or Whatsapp me @ 9888079179

4

TRIUMPHS & TRIALS IN THE ER

As "Life of a Doctor" progresses to Chapter 4, the spotlight shifts to the fast-paced world of the Emergency Room (ER). Dr. Atin finds himself at the epicentre of medical crises, where split-second decisions can mean the difference between life and death.

The chapter opens with the chaotic symphony of the ER – the blaring sirens, urgent footsteps, and the constant hum of medical equipment responding to emergencies ranging from traumas to critical illnesses. Each case becomes a unique challenge, a puzzle to solve under the relentless ticking of the clock.

Triumphs are celebrated, and trials are faced head-on in the ER. This chapter explores the emotional rollercoaster of high-stakes situations, the elation of successful interventions, and the weight of those moments when despite the best efforts, outcomes remain uncertain. Through Atin's eyes, readers witness the resilience required to navigate the unpredictable terrain of emergency medicine.

The camaraderie among ER staff becomes a focal point, emphasizing the importance of teamwork in a setting where every second counts. The relationships formed in the pressure cooker of the ER become a source of support, offering a lifeline amidst the relentless demands of the profession.

Amidst the chaos, the chapter also delves into the impact of these intense experiences on Atin's personal life. The blurred boundaries between work and home life, the constant exposure to trauma, and the emotional toll of being a healer in the ER are explored with a raw authenticity that resonates with readers.

As the chapter draws to a close, the ER becomes more than a workplace; it is a crucible where Atin hones his skills, confronts his fears, and discovers the strength within. The challenges faced and the lessons learned in this high-pressure environment set the stage for the next phase of Atin's journey in "Life of a Doctor."

Have you ever felt that rush of pride after helping someone in need? As doctors, we experience it every day.

I'll never forget the first time I truly felt that sense of accomplishment. I still remember the day vividly. It was my first night in ER of GMC Patiala. We received a message that there had been a head on collision of two buses just at the outskirts of Patiala and some NGO is helping them out and bringing the victims to our hospital. As I prepared myself for the situation my heart was racing and my hands were shaking ever so slightly. This was the moment I had worked so hard for, yet the weight of responsibility felt so heavy. As we received the traumatised patients which included all types of injury some with head injury some with cuts over face, arm, legs & some with tongue cuts. Resident in the ER told me 'Atin this is the time when world needs you, Pick up the surgical tray and go ahead, Help in what ever way you can'

I took a deep breath and made the first suture. With each careful movement of my scalpel, I gained more confidence. Hours later, I stepped back and realized the ER was settled. My patients were stable and recovering smoothly. A wave of pride and accomplishment washed over me.

"This made me recall when I first entered medical school. I was pursuing my lifelong dream of becoming a doctor and helping others. Though the road was long, I persevered through endless studying, gruelling residencies, and high-stress environments. My purpose kept me going – to make a difference in people's lives."

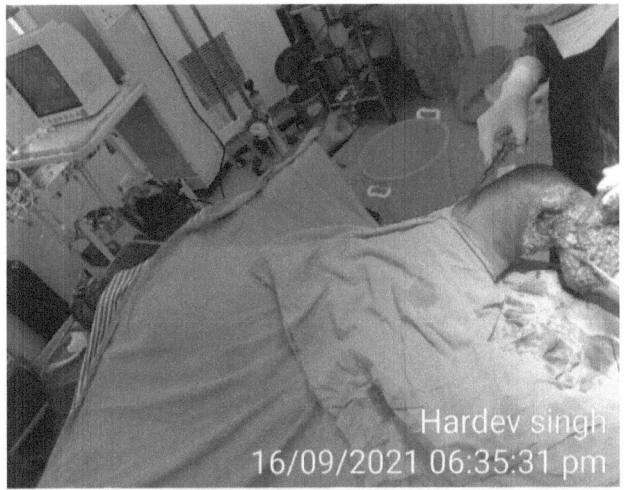

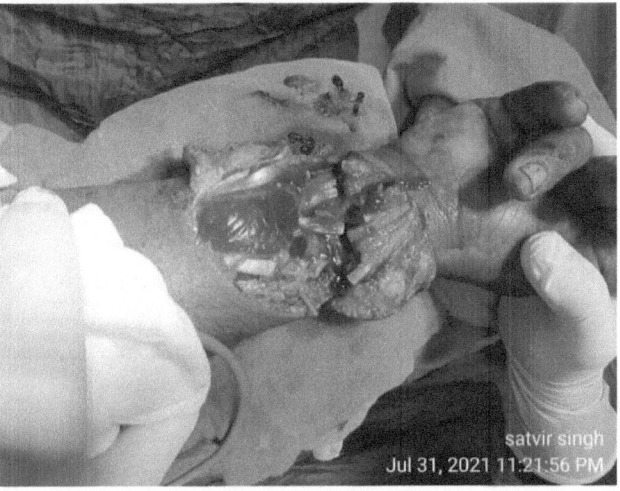

That day marked a major milestone in my medical career. Though I've performed countless procedures since, I'll never forget the exhilaration of that first experience of ER. It was the culmination of years of intense study and training, setting me on the path to becoming the doctor I am today.

The emotional rush of that moment is difficult to put into words. But any doctor remembers their first emergency procedure. It's a career-defining experience.

The narrative follows as Atin steps into the demanding realm of residency. The hallowed halls of medical school give way to the bustling corridors of the hospital, where life as a resident unfolds in a whirlwind of challenges and triumphs.

Residency marks a critical juncture in Atin's journey, a period of transition from theoretical knowledge to the practical application of medicine. Long hours, sleepless nights, and the relentless pace of patient care define this chapter, providing readers with an unfiltered look into the crucible where doctors are forged.

As Atin navigates various medical specialties during his residency, the reader is exposed to the multifaceted nature of healthcare. From the high-stakes drama of the emergency room to the precision required in surgery, each rotation shapes Atin's skills and contributes to the vast reservoir of experiences that will define him as a doctor.

The chapter also explores the delicate balance between professional commitments and personal well-being. The toll of long hours and demanding schedules weighs heavily on Atin and his colleagues, raising questions about the sustainability of a career in medicine. Yet, amidst the challenges, moments of camaraderie and shared purpose offer glimpses of the deep sense of fulfilment that keeps them going.

Through the trials and triumphs of residency, Atin's character is further melded, and his dedication to the art of healing is put to the test.

Did you know that doctors often have incredibly moving experiences that stay with them for the rest of their careers? As a doctor, you never forget the first time you save a life. That feeling of triumph and joy is unlike anything else.

Many of you reading this are doctors yourselves. You know that moment when a patient clings to life by a thread, and you pull them back from the brink. When their eyes open again and they thank you for giving them more time with their loved ones. That's a moment you'll never forget.

For me, that pivotal moment came during my first year of residency at MGM Medical College, Kamothe, Navi Mumbai. It was a great experience, working long shift in the ER. A man was rushed in with a massive heart attack. My team and I worked furiously, doing everything we could to save him. The minutes stretched on, like an eternity. And then finally, his heart started beating again. We had brought him back from the brink. I'll always remember the relief that washed over me when his vitals returned to normal. In that moment, I felt a profound validation of my calling. I remember Dr. Jayshree Ghanekar golden words 'Atin, *hard work pays off*'. Her mentorship had prepared me for this moment, gave me the confidence to trust my instincts, and the drive to keep honing my skills.

We all have these moments that shape us forever. I hope you never forget yours. It's those memories that get us through the long nights on call and remind us why we do what we do.

Each of us in medicine has our own "light bulb" moments — times when we realize how privileged of making a difference. Those moments are what make the long hours and stress worthwhile.

One such moment is when a seriously ill patient recovers under your care. As a doctor, you pour everything you have into treating patients. Seeing someone get better from the brink of death is an incredible feeling, knowing you made a difference and gave them more time with their family is hugely impactful.

These moments reminds us of our commitment. It reaffirms your conviction that you are in the right profession and your work matters. During tough times, you reflect on these proud moments and it re-energizes your passion. It's a privilege to be there for people during their most vulnerable times and make a positive impact.

After finishing my residency, I started working at Mahavir Dal Charitable Hospital in my hometown Bathinda, serving low-income families. Being a doctor instills a deep sense of social responsibility. I vividly remember my first patient — a single mother desperate to save her daughter from asthma attack.

We worked together with help of Ngo SAMARPAN, to ensure she received necessary aid. Witnessing their relief and gratitude was incredibly rewarding.

So, take a moment to reminisce about the first time you saved a life. Know that you've given that same feeling to patients countless times since— You are their hero.

If you're in medicine, or considering a career in healthcare take a moment to remember the "wins" that fill you with pride. We can't always save everyone, but when we do, it's the best feeling in the world.

My proudest moments as a doctor come from making a tangible difference in my patients' well-being. Whether it's an accurate diagnosis, compassionate care, or improved access to treatment, I find deep fulfilment in being there for people during vulnerable times. My journey has been long, but these moments of human connection make it all worthwhile.

I remember receiving a call from my friend Naresh Goyal in midnight, about his mother's difficulty in breathing. Urging him to bring her to the hospital, I arrived before them. His mother was in distress, I had no time to spare. I quickly split the work to Prinkal and Ravi, and sprang into action. We immediately intubated her, followed by emergency CPR. We gave the emergency drugs and with GOD's grace we were able to revive her. Alerting every one of her critical condition, we shifted her to cardiac hospital, while after a week, she made a remarkable recovery. While relaxing in my room I recalled that precious moment which made a difference in the life of whole family.

If you're a doctor, remember to appreciate the special moments when patients recover. Let it inspire you to keep giving your best. Your work can change lives, strive to create proud moments.

Have you ever had a moment that made you truly proud to be a doctor?

As medical professionals, we don't often take time to reflect on our accomplishments. Our days are filled with patient visits, reviewing test results, and managing a whirlwind of tasks..

But every so often, we have an experience that reminds us why we chose this path. A moment that makes us stands a little taller and thinks, "This is why I became a doctor."

One such moment happened a few years ago with a teenage patient named Harry, who was battling leukaemia. Despite multiple rounds of chemo, the cancer persisted, taking a toll on his vibrant life.

After discussing experimental drug therapy as an option, hope rekindled in their eyes, despite the chances being low.

Months later, Harry walked into my office for a follow-up visit. To my astonishment, his scans showed no sign of cancer. The experimental treatment had worked — a moment of overwhelming joy as Harry embraced me. I had to fight back tears of joy.

In that moment, it reinforced my purpose— to bring hope and healing even in the face of gruelling odds. To walk with them through life's darkest valleys and emerge together in the light.

The years of intense study, long hours on call, and high-stakes decisions —self-doubt inevitably creeps in. Have I chosen the right career? Can I handle the pressures and responsibilities? Am I making a difference?

Then a moment arrives that makes it all worthwhile. A colleague compliments your surgical technique. You diagnose a puzzling illness. A terminal patient squeezes your hand, thanking you for the extra time you spent. A child whose life you saved, graduates from college. These moments bring a profound sense of purpose and validation.

For doctors, the pressures and stresses of the job are counterbalanced by pride in serving and healing others. In the most difficult times, remembering the lives we've changed keeps us going. Though rewarding, a medical career requires resilience. But the pride we feel during those special moments gives meaning to our calling. Our skills and dedication matter – they save and change lives. We make a difference.

I'm sharing this story in appreciation of all my fellow physicians, nurses, and healthcare workers. Let's continue supporting each other through the highs and lows, celebrating the special moments that remind us our passion.

I'm curious to hear from fellow doctors. What was your first solo procedure like? What lessons have stayed with you today? Please share your stories and insights!

This chapter is for doctors, surgeons, and medical professionals who can relate to the journey of growth from fresh-faced resident to experienced physician. Let's reconnect with the passion that started us on this path.

I'm curious to hear from other doctors. What was your first solo procedure like? What lessons did you learn that still stick with you today? Please share your stories and insights below!

Write down to me what you feel @ My contact details: <u>authordratin@gmail.com</u> or Whatsapp me @ 9888079179

5

UNDERSTANDING FINANCIAL ASPECTS OF BEING A DOCTOR

By this time, I was a dedicated and compassionate physician who dreamed of becoming a doctor, inspired by the stories of healing and hope I read in my childhood. Fresh out of medical school, I was thrilled to start my career as a doctor. I had spent countless hours studying, training, and sacrificing to get to this point, however, was naive about the financial realities of being a doctor.

After years of rigorous study and training, I was excited to finish medical school and residency, finally achieving my dream. However, along with the joy of helping others came the realities of financial responsibility.

However, I was shocked by the mountain of debt.

The burden felt crushing, and despite having no savings I could barely cover my living expenses on my resident's salary. My budget was tighter than the scrubs I wore every day.

Each month, a significant portion of his income went towards loan payments, leaving him with little room for other expenses. Even after securing a stable job, financial struggle persist. Studies show nearly half of doctors feel "burned out" due to financial stress.

Doctors have a glamorized reputation for being well-off financially, with high salaries portraying as they are rolling in cash but the reality is more nuanced. It's not as easy as they make it seem. Doctors go through one of the longest training periods, often taking on huge debts. Their income also fluctuates wildly over their career making financial planning trickier. Despite good salary, they struggle with finding meaning beyond their work. They start earning later in life after years of low-paying or unpaid training associated with huge student loans, high insurance premiums, and the rising costs of running a practice. Yes, doctors have the potential to earn significant incomes, especially later in their careers. However, the road to get there requires major financial investments.

Establishing a practice requires significant start up costs and overhead. It takes time to build a patient base and revenue stream:

- Indemnity insurance premiums have skyrocketed, costing tens of thousands per year.

- Operating costs like staff, equipment, and overhead eat away at incomes. On-going licensing fees, equipment costs, and practice expenses persist.

- Doctors don't earn at peak levels until mid-career, often delayed until their 40s or 50s. After taxes and expenses, doctors' high salaries don't seem so high anymore.

Being a doctor is a noble profession, but it also comes with financial challenges. Managing money wisely is crucial. Despite the financial strain, I found fulfilment in work, knowing that I was making a difference in the lives of my patients. But as the years went by, I realized the importance of planning for my financial future.

In this chapter, I'll discuss the financial ups and downs doctors face and provide tips for managing money wisely while leading a fulfilling life. Most people believe doctors are wealthy. While doctors earn a good income, their finances can be complex. Student loans, insurance, investments must be managed well.

Most medical students graduate with a debt. Imagine starting your career with that financial burden!

With such high debt, it's no wonder many doctors feel trapped in unfulfilling jobs just to pay the bills. They question if it was worth the sacrifices. Some even experience depression and burnout.

But it doesn't have to be this way. With smart strategies, you can pay off loans, save for the future, and create work-life balance. You can find purpose beyond the pay check. Doctors have unique financial situations. With intentional money management, they can achieve financial success.

Wouldn't it be great to pay off debt quickly, invest wisely, and have more freedom in your career — while also leading a life you love outside of work? By optimizing finances and reframing priorities, it is possible!

Here are 3 steps doctors can take to improve finances and increase fulfilment:

1. Make a debt repayment plan: Talk to a financial advisor about the fastest way to pay off student loans. Consider loan consolidation and refinancing.

2. Live below your means: Avoid the trap of inflating your lifestyle to match your income. Find ways to save on housing, transportation, and discretionary spending.

3. Reassess your values: What really matters most to you? Look for ways to incorporate meaning into your medical career, such as teaching, research, global health, or policy work.

With intentional effort, you can reduce money stress and create a career and life you love. What step will you take? There are ways doctors can get ahead financially. Refinancing student loans, living frugally, and investing wisely early on can make a big difference. Seeking good advisors to create smart financial plans is the key. With the right moves, doctors can pay off loans faster, build assets, and gain control over their finances. Though the path is tough, with diligence doctors can find financial freedom.

I sought advice from a financial planner, who helped me to create a budget and prioritize my financial goals. Together, we developed a plan to pay off the student loans while also saving for retirement and building an emergency fund. Through careful budgeting and planning, I paid off my loans in five years while maximizing retirement savings. This was possible with meticulous planning of financial advisers Mr. Rakesh and Mrs. Sunaina Garg from Smartway Investments. As my career progressed, my income grew, allowing me to pay off my debts faster and invest in the future. It diversified my investments, putting money into stocks, bonds, and real estate to build wealth over time.

I also invested in disability insurance and indemnity coverage to protect myself and my assets. I understood the importance of insuring myself against unforeseen circumstances that could threaten my livelihood.

Despite the financial challenges of being a doctor, I found a balance between my work and personal life. I made time for my family and hobbies, knowing that well-being was just as important as my career success.

Through careful planning and dedication, I achieved financial stability and security. I continued to practice medicine with passion and purpose, knowing that my financial future was in good hands.

The bottom line is with smart strategies, doctors can overcome financial hurdles and achieve their wealth-building goals. But it takes intentional effort. The financial finish line may seem far off, but with perseverance, doctors can get there.

Another reason is Doctors often don't pay enough attention to their personal finances. With long hours and demanding work, it's easy to neglect money management, but finances are a critical part of life. Throughout their careers, doctors must understand tax optimization, retirement planning, insurance, and investing to build wealth properly.

Handling finances wisely is vital for doctors to achieve financial freedom, fund major goals like buying a home, and retire comfortably. Without diligence in money management, doctors risk serious financial stress or running out of money later in life.

Doctors should make finances a priority. They should craft a financial plan early on, work with financial advisors as I did with Smart way Investments and regularly review their money situation. Key actions include paying off high-interest debt, taking advantage of tax deductions, maximizing retirement accounts, and investing wisely. Good financial habits will pay off hugely long-term.

Take control of your finances today! With smart planning and discipline, you can secure your financial future. But also being the soft targets, doctors need to be vigilant while investing. Online frauds, risky investments in crypto, short term gains are something which can loot your hard earned money.

The financial life of a doctor is a long game requiring perseverance. While the potential for high earnings exists, the road to get there is filled with challenges. Patience and financial planning are critical early on.

After 10+ gruelling years of education, doctors enter the workforce shackled with six-figure student loans before making their first income

This impacts all of us. High medical school costs get passed onto patients through higher medical bills and insurance premiums. And financially strained doctors experience burnout, depression, and suicidal thoughts at alarming rates.

But there is hope. The government is expanding programs that forgive loans for working in underserved areas. And doctors are speaking out about the need for reform.

We all have a stake in fixing this broken system. Medical school costs are unsustainable for aspiring doctors and harmful to the patients they care for. The health of our nation depends on it.

Building wealth doesn't happen overnight, but by making smart financial choices over time, I now have a level of financial freedom and stability. Now, since I am happily married, I can also bear the extra expenses that come with it like buying expensive gift for my wife Deepali, looking ahead for a better education perspectives for my kids Anirudh and Manit, and also take care of my father Dr. Pawan K. Gupta, who with the hard work and dedication helped me reach this point. I can party out with my friends, roam in an expensive car and go out for holidays for both national and international trips.

With focus and discipline, it is possible to get out of debt, save and invest wisely, and achieve financial goals. I had to learn this through trial and error at the beginning of my career. By sharing my experience, I can help other doctors in their financial journeys. The long hours caring for patients are worth it when you take control of your finances.

Are you also suffering from financial crunch? Share with me your problems and I would definitely be more than happy to help you and make you come out of the financial burden. If you have expertise supporting doctor's financials, share your knowledge.

Hope this chapter has provided a candid look into the financial life of a doctor. It dispels myths and provides real solutions.

Write down to me for any financial assistance @ My contact details: <u>authordratin@gmail.com</u> or Whatsapp me @ 9888079179

6

COMMITMENTS TO CONTINUING MEDICAL EDUCATION

The Lifeline for Doctors' Careers

Doctors have one of the most demanding yet rewarding careers. After graduating from medical school and completing residency, many think the intensive education is over. However, with medicine constantly evolving, learning never stops for physicians. Medical knowledge doubles every 73 days. Treatments that were standard a few years ago can quickly become obsolete as new research emerges. Continuing Medical Education (CME) is essential for providing excellent patient care throughout a doctor's career. CME allows doctors to stay current on the latest evidence-based practices, medications, technologies, and more. It is key to improving patient outcomes in an ever-changing healthcare landscape. CME takes many forms, including conferences, grand rounds, online courses, and reading peer-reviewed journals. While some view this as a chore, many appreciate CME as an opportunity to deepen their expertise and connect with colleagues.

Lifelong learning is fulfilling as it allows physicians to expand their knowledge, advance their skills, and provide the best possible care to patients. Although medical school graduation leads to MD or DO degrees, the learning does not stop there. Doctors have an ethical duty through CME to continuously enhance their abilities over the decades of their careers.

CME enables doctors to be the best clinicians they can be. It is an essential and enriching part of a physician's journey of professional development and excellence.

How often do doctors need to update their skills? More than you think! Unlike most careers, a medical degree is not a "one-and-done" qualification.

In fact, CME is mandatory for doctors to maintain their licenses. Doctors must complete a certain number of CME credits each year to maintain their medical license. On average, doctors must complete 10 hours of CME every year. That's because medicine is rapidly evolving as new technologies, treatments, medications, and research emerges. What doctors learned in medical school years ago may have become outdated or obsolete. The CME requirement for credit hours is just the tip of the iceberg. On top of that, you read medical journals, attend conferences, take certification exams, and seek out mentors. Lifelong learning is essential to providing the best possible care to patients.

For example, my friend Dr. Anjali, who is a pediatrician, shared how much childhood nutrition recommendations have changed over the past decade based on new studies. Without regular CME, she wouldn't be giving the most up-to-date feeding advice to parents. As the President Elect for IAP, Punjab 2025, shares that doctors and pediatricians in particular, who are taking care of the new lives, need to remain updated about the recent advances in the ever-evolving medical field.

CME looks different for every doctor based on their speciality, which may be clinical, para-clinical or non-clinical. It includes reading medical journals, attending conferences, taking online courses, and more. The goal is to fill in gaps in knowledge without compromising the patient's care.

Some doctors view CME as a chore, but many see it as fascinating and even fun — like earning a mini-degree every year! One thing is certain: CME keeps doctors sharp and patients safer. The next time you see your physician, remember how hard they work to stay on top of medicine's ever-changing landscape.

Doctors have a professional obligation to keep up with the latest medical knowledge. But with the explosion of new research and treatments, how can they find time?

According to one survey, most doctors spend only fifteen hours per year on continuing medical education (CME). Yet medical knowledge doubles every 18 months and this gap is concerning.

I have been an internist for 20 years, running my own Indrani Multispecialty Hospital providing state-of-the-art facilities for critically ill patients. I feel proud on providing evidence-based care. But lately, I noticed some of my practices are out dated as my patients sometimes mention new treatments I haven't heard of. I want to stay on trend, but struggle to find time for CME with my busy practice. After completing my post-graduation, I pursued additional training in 2D-Echo, earned a Post Graduate Diploma in Diabetes Mellitus, and completed a Fellowship in Dialysis.

Every doctor faces this constant problem: keeping their medical knowledge and skills up to date. New research, technologies, treatments and best practices emerge every day. This endless influx of new medical knowledge can quickly make a physician's training obsolete. Without continuing education, doctors can fall behind in standards of care. Patients suffer the consequences of outdated medical practices.

The sheer volume of new medical literature published each year is staggering. One estimate suggests that for a doctor to keep up with the research in their specialty, they would have to read for 627 hours per year – almost 2 hours every day! And CME requirements continue to grow as medical boards and hospitals demand more education credits to maintain licensure and privileges. This continuing medical education (CME) can feel like an overwhelming burden on top of an already demanding career.

Doctors owe it to their patients to dedicate time for continuing education. But with the demands on their time, creative solutions are needed. Medical associations, hospitals, and training institutes need to make high-quality CME more accessible. The gap between new advances and applied practice needs to shrink.

The constant need to stay on top of new research and guidelines can be hard and burn out anyone.

That's why continuing medical education (CME) is so vital for physicians. CME allows doctors to keep their skills sharp and prevent career stagnation. Through CME, doctors can:

- Learn about new treatment options and medical technologies

- Brush up on latest clinical guidelines and protocols

- Understand impacts of healthcare legislation and reforms

- Gain insights from colleagues during conferences and seminars

- Expand their professional network and find mentors

CME keeps doctors engaged and enthusiastic about their work, it recharges their passion for healing others. Doctors who regularly pursue CME provide higher quality care and have greater career satisfaction. They are lifelong learners who thrive on intellectual growth. It enables doctors to stay current in their field and ensures physicians have access to the latest medical research and clinical data. It also allows doctors to learn new skills, adopt best practices and provide optimal patient care. When doctors regularly participate in CME, they deliver higher quality care. Patients benefit from up-to-date treatment based on recent scientific advances.

This constant pressure to learn can lead to doctor burnout. CME often means sacrificing personal time to pore over dry medical journals or attend conferences on weekends and vacations. The demands are daunting, especially for doctors just establishing their careers.

Is there really no other way?

The good news is that technology now allows for more convenient, engaging continuing education. Online CME courses let doctors learn on their own schedule. Podcasts and videos deliver bite-sized learning during commutes or downtime. And interactive virtual conferences connect doctors to the latest insights without the hassle of travel.

Continuing education may feel like a burden, but it doesn't have to be. With the right approach, doctors can stay up-to-date efficiently and even enjoy the process of lifelong learning. The medical field will always evolve, but technology gives doctors new tools to master that evolution while still living a balanced life. The ideal of the all-knowing physician may be unrealistic, but with modern CME, competency and great patient care are still within every doctor's reach.

Dr Deepali, my partner, despite taking care of her private diagnostic centre and fulfilling her responsibilities at home, takes out time for attending CME's to be upgraded in her routine practice, which has helped her to build a reputation of expertise in the field of oncopathology. Her reports are accepted even at higher centres of oncology. This is what is satisfying and encourages you to always keep learning, which is a demand of the profession and also part of medical ethics.

First, be aware that CME is a professional and ethical responsibility. Medical boards and licensing organizations across the world require physicians to complete a certain number of CME credits annually as part of maintaining licensure. While mandatory CME aims to ensure physicians are up-to-date, you should also recognize the intrinsic value of regularly educating yourself. Make CME a priority not just for compliance, but also for your patients.

Next, comprehend how CME benefits your practice. Through CME, you gain exposure to new technologies, treatment guidelines, research, and best practices. This translates to better diagnostic capabilities, more effective treatments, and improved patient outcomes. Patients expect and deserve to be treated by knowledgeable doctors utilizing the latest evidence-based approaches. Regular CME allows you to deliver on that expectation.

Then, convince yourself that consistent but manageable CME is feasible. With online courses, podcasts, journals, conferences, and more CME options than ever before, you can find convenient ways to fit learning into a busy schedule. By dedicating just a few hours each week, you can continuously build your expertise. View CME as an investment in sharpening your clinical skills and providing exceptional care.

Finally, take action by setting CME goals for this year. Outline topics you want to strengthen, modalities to explore, and a plan for staying accountable. Let CME reinforce your passion for medicine by enhancing your capabilities. Lifelong learning is a hallmark of a consummate physician. Make it a priority and see how regular education positively impacts your practice and patients.

The takeaway? Embrace CME as a professional obligation and a lifelong journey. It enables you to practice at the top of your license by equipping you with the latest clinical knowledge and skills. Staying educated pays dividends to you and your patients.

If you're a doctor seeking to reignite your passion, make CME a priority. Set a goal to complete a certain number of CME credits annually. Seek out education that aligns with your professional interests and helps you be the best physician possible. Your patients will benefit, and your career will thank you.

Some novel ideas include micro-learning apps, online CME courses during downtime, and hospital-sponsored education stipends. There are options, if we get creative. You can also find a place in your own city. As in our city, Bathinda, we have a Physician forum, which is very active. I am an active member of the forum. I had been the secretary twice and not only took interest in learning and updating, but also conducted the CME's for my fellow colleagues promoting the advancement in the medical field. The most effective CME focuses on your specific needs and interests within your specialty.

Seek out personalized, practice-relevant CME that bridges gaps in knowledge, helps you implement new guidelines, and improves patient outcomes. Choose activities that fit your schedule and learning style, too.

At the end of the day, continuing education is fulfilling. It sparks intellectual curiosity, sharpens critical thinking, and keeps you engaged. While the medical knowledge base expands exponentially, lifelong learning helps you keep pace. Most importantly, it allows you to give your patients the excellent care they deserve.

Continuing education is a professional necessity for physicians. CME transforms medical knowledge into better health outcomes. The most skilled doctors never stop learning. They recognize that regular CME enables them to offer the best possible care to patients. Lifelong learning is imperative in the ever-changing field of medicine. With the constant influx of new research, technologies, and best practices, medicine is a field that requires lifelong learning.

How do you keep up with the latest medical advances? What CME approaches have you found effective and time-efficient? Please share your experiences and ideas below.

This chapter is aimed at doctors, nurses, healthcare administrators, medical association leaders, and other medical professionals. Let's work together to close the continuing education gap. Our patients are counting on us.

Write down to me for any updates in this ever evolving world @ My contact details: authordratin@gmail.com or Whatsapp me @ 9888079179

7

BALANCING PROFESSIONAL AND PERSONAL LIFE: KEY INSIGHTS

As a doctor, your patients rely on you. You have committed your life to caring for others, but what about caring for yourself? Finding balance between your demanding career and personal life can feel impossible. Doctors are responsible for the health and wellbeing of their patients - an immense responsibility that requires long hours, being constantly on-call, and making difficult decisions. But doctors are still humans, with their own needs for work-life balance. So how can doctors find that elusive balance between their careers and their personal lives?

Being a doctor is incredibly demanding. Emergencies come up unexpectedly. It's easy to let your job take over everything else. The weekend shifts, and being constantly on-call can make it hard to find time for yourself and your loved ones. Many doctors struggle to achieve work-life balance, leading to burnout, exhaustion, and poor mental health over time. The stress of making life-or-death decisions, and the constant pressure to perform can take a major toll.

The struggle is real, but work-life balance is possible in medicine. However, with some effort and creativity, you can find more harmony between your demanding career and your precious personal life.

Having a life outside of medicine is so important for your mental and physical health. Making time for family, friends, hobbies, exercise, and self-care can help prevent burnout and compassion fatigue. A balanced life will ultimately make you a happier, healthier, and more effective doctor.

Achieving work-life balance is crucial, yet challenging. How can you make time for exercise, hobbies, friends, family, and self-care when your patients always need you? Is it even possible to find work-life balance as a doctor when lives are on the line? The demands of the job never stop. Something's got to give. But what? Your career? Your relationships? Your health? There are no easy answers.

We need to normalize prioritizing work-life balance in the medical profession. Reducing stigmas around taking vacations, taking sick days when needed, and setting boundaries will benefit both doctors and patients. We can't pour from an empty cup.

While there are no perfect solutions, there are ways to create more harmony between your work and personal life. Set boundaries and limit working overtime. Take all your vacation days. Make time for date nights and activities you enjoy. Consider part-time scheduling if possible. Build a support network of family and friends to help out. Find physician groups to connect with about maintaining work-life balance. Consider hiring home services to reduce chores. Make self-care a priority, whether it's exercise, meditation, or therapy. Achieving more work-life balance takes effort and intention, but it's worth it. A happier, healthier you will be a better doctor in the long run.

Start small. Block out time for the people and activities you love. Take a lunch break, leave work on time, and let go of guilt. Your health and relationships are worth protecting. Together, we can shift the culture to promote sustainable careers in medicine. It starts with making self-care and your needs a priority too. You've got this! Doctors who find balance between work and life are happier, healthier, and more effective in caring for patients. They have lower rates of burnout and are able to sustain their careers over the long-term.

I remember my first year of residency at MGM Medical College, working 36 to 60-hour shifts and collapsing from exhaustion. My health and relationships suffered. I lost significant weight in my first fifteen days of residency. I was eating just to avoid further weight loss and sleeping in shifts just to regain my energy to work again. My mother called to discuss my marriage life. I was not able to think beyond my duties and add another responsibility on my shoulders. I thought there weren't just enough hours in the day to be the doctor and still have time for yourself and your loved ones.

After one too many long-hour shifts, I realized I needed to make some changes. So how do doctors manage it all? What are the tips and tricks?

I spoke with Dr. Deepali, my better half, to give her perspective. She's a renowed oncopathologist, runs her own centre under the name 'Dr Deepali Path Labs' and is also a mother of two. She shared how she structures her life to make time for both work and family. She has scheduled her appointments when the kids are out for school. She is home to have lunch with them, manages their homework and study time, and oversees extracurricular activities. Despite managing the family, she takes out time for herself by going to the fitness club and socializing with her neighbours, apart from her dedication to the medical profession.

A key strategy is being intentional about boundaries. Dr. Deepali is careful to fully disconnect from work when she's home. She doesn't answer emails or take calls. Those are reserved for office hours. She also blocks out family time on her calendar, treating it as seriously as a patient appointment.

She prepares healthy meals in advance and gets exercise when she can. She's honest with her kids when work pulls her focus. But she's fully present with them when she's home.

So it starts with setting boundaries and being disciplined about maintaining them. It also means taking care of your own health —eating well, exercising, and getting enough sleep. Self-care is essential.

Another key is having a strong support system at home. A partner who truly understands the demands and is willing to share the load makes a huge difference. If you have children, secure reliable childcare. Don't be afraid to ask for help. Spending time with family and friends during the season or watching sports activities.

Watching T-20 with family

Celebrating Teachers Day with Best Teacher

Tuffman Marathon 10km

At work, communicate openly with colleagues about the need for balance. See if you can share or adjust schedules to accommodate family needs. If your workplace culture doesn't support balance, consider a different practice. There are options out there.

Most importantly, remember that while your patients depend on you, your own family does too. Make them a priority. Set an example for other doctors that balance is possible with intention, boundaries and self-care. A fulfilled doctor is best able to fulfill their calling.

I started setting firm boundaries with my time. I don't schedule any work appointments before 8 a.m. and after 6 p.m., so I can have time to exercise, connect with friends, and relax. I take my full lunch break to recharge. I divert my phone after hours and on weekends. If I need extra coverage for personal time, I ask colleagues to swap shifts.

The result? I have more energy and feel less burned out. My connections outside of work are stronger. I'm able to be fully present with patients during the day. The key for me was being intentional about prioritizing my needs. I encourage you to reflect on what brings you joy and how to create space for that. You'll be a better doctor and person for it.

Did you know that nearly half of all physicians report burnout symptoms? That startling statistic comes from a study by the Mayo Clinic Proceedings. With long hours and immense pressure, it's no wonder doctors struggle to find work-life balance.

I changed my lifestyle, which had been instrumental in my overall development. I would like to share the Silver Jubilee of our MBBS'99 batch. It was a great responsibility where we had to set aside extra time despite our routine duties, life style, and our commitments with family and friends. At this time, Dr. ANJALI (my batch mate) , Dr. DEEPALI (my better half), and my best friend Dr. ROHIT helped me accomplish the whole event hassle free. Nothing is possible individually. Our other batch mates to mention Bhavneet, Meenu, Parvinder, Ritu, Puneet, Ratika and Manisha from Patiala, Mansa, Delhi, and Jalandhar all took out their special time to make the event a grand success. We shared our experiences and pondered about the future in the medical field. After 25 years, we all found balance in our personal and professional lives. I would like to mention about my friend Kamal and Priyanka, despite having a family situation, they arrived. A Special mention goes to Blossom, Natasha, and Navjot who travelled from distant places. Moments of connection and reflection are crucial for maintaining a balanced life.

. Here are a few tips that helped me achieve work-life balance:

- Set boundaries and limit work hours. Even starting small makes a difference.

- Take time for yourself every day, like 15 minutes of meditation or a quick walk. Give your mind and body a break.

- Build support networks, whether it's loved ones who understand your schedule or colleagues who you can vent to. Don't try to cope alone.

- Take advantage of flexibility at work, adjust your schedule or work remotely.

- Consider part-time work or job sharing, to reduce your workload.

- Make time for non-work hobbies and relationships.

- Don't skip vacations. Use all your paid time off for rest and rejuvenation.

- Have a life outside medicine. Cultivate personal relationships and interests other than the job.

- Practice self-care. Eat well, exercise, and get enough sleep, so you have energy for all parts of your life.

Achieving greater balance between a demanding career and a fulfilling personal life takes intention and effort. But it pays off tremendously, allowing you to be at your best both at work and at home. Also doctors who find balance are happier, healthier, and more effective in caring for patients, with lower rates of burnout and sustainable careers.

The reality is, balancing a medical career with personal life is an on-going challenge. But taking active steps to prioritize yourself and protect your time can help you avoid burnout. We owe it to ourselves and our patients to practice self-care. Our health and happiness depend on it.

How do you maintain work-life balance despite a demanding medical career?

What are your best tips for balancing work and life as a doctor? Share your thoughts below!

Let me know if you have any other tips for finding balance! I'm still learning.

What are your tips for achieving work-life balance in medicine? How do you make time for yourself and your loved ones? Let's share ideas and support each other.

This chapter is for physicians, residents, medical students, and healthcare professionals seeking work-life balance. We're in this together.

Write down to me for any suggestions @ My contact details: authordratin@gmail.com or Whatsapp me @ 9888079179

8

MANAGING STRESS AND PRESSURE IN MEDICAL PRACTICE

The Pressure Cooker Life of a Doctor

Do you ever feel like you're drowning in stress? That no matter how hard you tread the water, the waves keep crashing over you? For doctors, this is an all-too-familiar feeling.

The life of a doctor is filled with unimaginable stress. From gruelling hours during medical school and residency to the pressures of making life-or-death decisions daily, doctors carry an enormous weight on their shoulders that few can comprehend.

Medical school is no joke. The sheer amount of information you need to cram into your brain is staggering. Anatomy, physiology, biochemistry, pharmacology — the list goes on. Not to mention the long hours shadowing physicians and working in hospitals. It's a pressure cooker environment.

The sacrifices doctors make start early. Medical school alone cost very high and last four intense years with 80+ hour study weeks. Then comes 3–7 years of residency, working 80-100+ hours per week. They miss holidays, birthdays, weddings — precious life moments all in service of their craft.

Even after residency, the pressures don't relent. Doctors must make split-second high-stakes decisions daily that impact human lives. A misdiagnosis or small mistake in surgery can be fatal. They deal with grieving families and work in chaotic ERs. Their mental health suffers as a result. Studies show physicians have higher rates of burnout and depression than the general population. According to research, doctors are at much higher risk for depression, substance abuse, and suicide compared to the general population.

The problem is clear — medical professionals operate under immense pressure on a daily basis, making life-altering decisions. As professionals, many of us deal with high pressure environments and stressful workloads. But few careers face the intense demands placed on physicians.

It's no wonder physicians have among the highest suicide rates of any profession. This is a disturbing and heart breaking reality. As caregivers for patients, they don't find time to self-care.

The gruelling years of medical training are just the beginning. Doctors must make life-and-death decisions every day, facing indemnity risks, dealing with difficult patients, and working in irregular hours. All while trying to maintain a work-life balance.

Stress is unavoidable in medicine, but burnout isn't. Prioritizing self-care and work-life balance helps doctors thrive in this demanding field.

There are solutions. We can advocate for reduced administrative burdens, better self-care resources, increase flexibility, and reasonable work hours. Most importantly, we must recognize the silent struggles. Offer compassion and understanding, remind them their lives matter too.

Prioritizing self-care is the key. If you're feeling burnt out, you're not alone. Reach out to colleagues or your physician health program. Evaluate ways to incorporate more balance day-to-day. With some changes, you can continue helping patients while also caring for yourself.

You've probably noticed how your doctor always seems stressed out and overworked. It's time we lift the burden and give them the support they deserve. Their wellbeing and our healthcare depend on it.

Doctors have to juggle a huge number of responsibilities. They diagnose illnesses, prescribe treatment plans, perform surgeries, manage staff, deal with insurance companies, keep up with the latest research — all while trying to spend enough time with each patient. No wonder they're always rushing around looking harried!

The stakes are also extremely high in their profession. Even small mistakes can have serious consequences. This means they have to be 100% focused every single day. There's no room for errors when lives are on the line.

As a doctor myself, I have a unique insider's view into the daily challenges doctors face in managing stress.

I remember one ER shift, we had multiple trauma patients come in after a serious car accident. My team and I had to jump into action immediately to assess injuries, stop bleeding, order tests, provide emergency treatment, and coordinate care. It was controlled chaos for hours. Although we saved lives that day, we also lost a young patient. The emotional impact hit me hard, but I had to compartmentalize and care for other critical patients. It was an emotionally and physically draining day that exemplified the intense stress inherent in this profession.

Another unforgettable era is of COVID. On a lighter note, do you know, dear friends, first phase of COVID came out as COVID:THE BEGINNING, and second phase as COVID:THE RISE, comparative to movie like 'PUSHPA'.

I, Dr. Atin, the nodal officer and in charge of COVID at Indrani Hospital, first in Bathinda, to start COVID facility. It was a time when there was no formal relationship. We would just receive a call from a fellow friend stating that they have a patient with Covid positive and send them in and ambulance. Since there was a lockdown, they couldn't accompany the patient but asked me to take care of them. This was a time where we had to choose between stress/pressure and responsibility. There was an immense pressure from family, friends, and dear ones to refrain from treating Covid patients, as it's a life threatening disease. On the other side, the feeling of responsibility, stating that this is what we have studied for, this is the time world needs us, this is the time you can feel proud like a soldier who is on forefront to protect lives, risking your own.

Pressure were also imbued from the government authorities, because of reporting cases, sending data, request for drugs like *Remdesevir*, and most importantly, to fulfil demand of oxygen supply. I still remember that dreaded day when we received a message from the appropriate authorities that liquid oxygen supply has been shut down due to transport issues, leaving us with last 10hrs of oxygen supply. I couldn't decide what to do for patients who are on high=flow oxygen with requirements touching up to more than 30L/hour. They would merely die within 15mins without sufficient oxygen, which otherwise were salvageable. That was a point of extreme stress when I had to call the relatives of the admitted patients to inform about the current situation.

I requested them to take their patient, as I couldn't witness all the deaths. While informing the guardians, a sense of shiver ran down my body, with tear in my eyes, and had a complete emotional breakdown. At that time, I received what was required the most: courage from family, and the relatives of the patients, who said *'Don't worry Doctor Saheb, We are with you, We will try to arrange the oxygen cylinders, you just continue treatment, your efforts are commendable'*. I think that Is all we require to get rid of all the pressure, the stresses, the burden we feel.

And this is what people reward you for. The case of Mrs. Nirmala devi, who was admitted during Covid, rewarded all our staff members who cared for her. There were many rewards for the stressful situation. I was also awarded by the then FM Sr. Manpreet Singh Badal for my services in COVID.

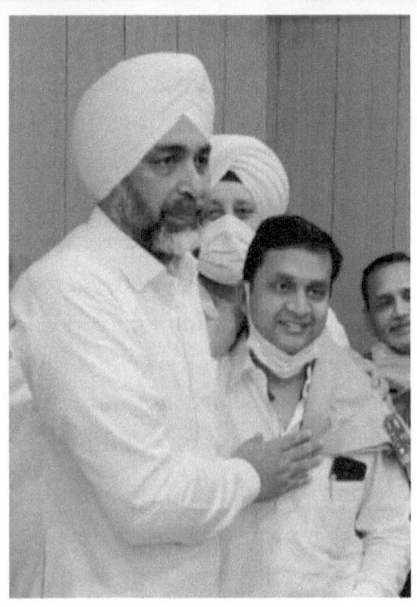

LIFE is stressful for everyone. Another incidence that comes to my mind is admission of Mr. Naresh Monga, owner of Mahindra agency, during COVID times. He was teetering between death and life, and in meanwhile, there was a big fire explosion at his work place. It was just impossible to inform him about the tragic event because it would have made him more despondent. Slowly, as his condition improved, he was informed about the loss. Life is not easy as it seems. Hardships are part of life and we need to come out of it.

Next time you see your family physician looking weary, remember that their job is infinitely tougher than most other professions.Appreciate the efforts doctors put in to keep YOU healthy. Their job is enormously demanding.

Let's try to make things a bit easier for them. We can show up on time for appointments, clearly communicate symptoms, follow their instructions carefully, and not burden them with unrealistic expectations. Little thoughtful gestures like a thank you card or positive review can also brighten their day during stressful times.

The next time you visit your doctor, make an effort to be patient and understanding. Ask them how their day is going and offer words of encouragement. Together, we can create a supportive environment for our physicians to help them manage the intense pressures of this demanding, but noble profession.

Remember the sacrifices they made to be there for you. Give them grace, understanding and patience. Their job is enormously difficult but vitally important.

We owe them tremendous gratitude for carrying the immense weight of our lives on their shoulders. They are true everyday heroes.

The medical school pressure cooker forges strong, compassionate, dedicated physicians. It's tough, but you'll look back one day with gratitude for the journey that made you the doctor you are. To all aspiring physicians, know that you have what it takes. Stay focused on the end goal, take care of yourself along the way, and you'll get there. Your patients are waiting for you.

It's all worth it on the other side. As a physician, you have the profound privilege of helping people every day. There's no greater feeling than using your hard-earned knowledge and skills to improve someone's health and wellbeing.

How do you cope with stress in your profession? What tips have worked for you? I'd love to hear your experiences in the comments!

This is for doctors and medical professionals dealing with burnout and work-related stress. I aim to provide solidarity and spark discussion on this important issue.

Write down to me for any type of help @ My contact details: authordratin@gmail.com or Whatsapp me @ 9888079179

9

BUILDING RELATIONSHIPS: PATIENT INTERACTIONS

Doctors, How Well Do You Really Know You're Patients?

In the busy day-to-day of a medical practice, it can be easy to lose sight of the human element. But for many physicians, connecting with patients on a personal level is one of the most meaningful parts of the job.

How well do you truly know the people sitting across from you during a check-up or procedure? As physicians, we spend our days diagnosing illnesses and developing treatment plans. But how often do we take a step back to understand our patients as whole people?

Getting to know your patients on a more personal level can transform their healthcare experience. Taking a few extra minutes to ask about their job, family, hobbies or passions shows you care for more than just their medical chart. Understanding patients' lifestyles and priorities helps you provide tailored care that aligns with their goals.

I'll never forget the first time I truly understood the power of these relationships. Early in my career, I was treating a teenage patient who was going through a rough patch and struggling with some unhealthy habits. I talked to him as if I were a friend. After obtaining consent from his parents to speak with him one-on-one, we had a heartfelt conversation. I learned about his hobbies, shared some of my own, we learned about our shared passion over cricket, changing the dynamics of our interactionhis problem was more than 50% resolved .

Over time, he began opening up to me in ways he hadn't before. Our check-ups turned into rich conversations where he'd share what was really going on in his life. This seeded a sliver of trust that allowed a doctor–patient bond to flourish.

WON IMA BTI TORNAMENT IN FEB 2021 WON IMA BTI TORNAMENT IN MARCH 2023

Making connections enables you to become partners in your patients' health rather than just clinicians. You gain insight into factors impacting their wellbeing and can collaborate on solutions. Patients feel respected, understood and invested in their care plan when you know them as individuals. While medicine has become more impersonal in some ways, moments of real human connection remain at the heart of what we do. Making space for them, even when we're pressed for time, can have an enormous impact. As caregivers, we have a profound opportunity to know our patients and vice versa. Those relationships are often what make the difficult days worthwhile.

As a young medical student, I was focused on acing exams and attaining clinical skills. I didn't realize how important patient interactions would be in my career.

Now as an attending physician with over a decade of experience, the patient relationships are what I look forward to each day. I've laughed with patients over shared stories, cried with them during difficult diagnoses, and celebrated their recoveries. We have even celebrated birthdays with cake cutting. Seeing their smiling faces and getting hugs in the hospital halls is the best part of my job.

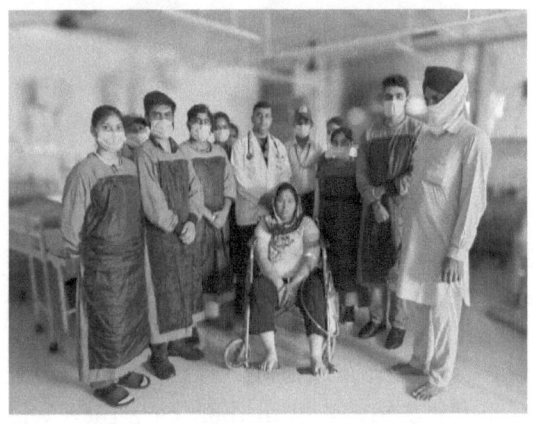

The Problem Physicians Face When Interacting With Patients

As a doctor, having good bedside manners is crucial for building trust and rapport with patients. However, in today's healthcare system, the demands on a physician's time often make meaningful patient interactions challenging.

Doctors are required to see more patients in less time. Appointment slots are shortened to squeeze in as many patients as possible. Electronic health records take physicians' attention away from the patient. Insurance restrictions limit what doctors can do or say.

With all these pressures, it's easy for physicians to limit their interactions with patients. Patients may feel like just another number instead of receiving the individual care and attention they expect and deserve. This breakdown in the doctor-patient relationship has consequences for the quality of care and patient satisfaction.

The Solution: Renew Focus on Compassion and Communication

To overcome the barriers to positive patient interactions, doctors need to renew their focus on compassion, empathy and communication. The patient-doctor relationship is the cornerstone of healthcare. As doctors, how we interact with patients can have a profound impact on their health outcomes. Simple steps like allowing extra time with patients, minimizing distractions, making eye contact, and being uninterrupted can go a long way. This not only helps achieve better results but also builds trust between patients and doctors in today's era. Doctors must build rapport, listen attentively, empathize, and explain complex information in a way patients can understand. Poor communication can lead to misdiagnoses, a lack of adherence to treatment plans, and patient dissatisfaction. Just hearing compassionately and explaining the disease properly can reduce mistrust and conflict in hospitals which have become common.

Effective patient communication requires skills that go beyond medical expertise. Doctors should also prioritize continuing education on topics like delivering difficult news, motivational interviewing, cultural competency, and shared decision-making. Sharpening these "soft skills" is just as important as keeping up with the latest medical advances.

To improve patient interactions, we can focus on honing our communication skills. Look for opportunities to make personal connections with patients before diving into medical discussions. Use plain language instead of complex jargon. Encourage patients to express their concerns and preferences openly. Schedule adequate time with each patient. When patients feel respected and heard, they entrust us with the immense responsibility of caring for their well-being.

Health systems should support physicians by allowing longer appointments when needed, hiring ancillary staff, and providing training on communication and relationship-building. Improving patient interactions will lead to better health outcomes, reduce physician burnout, and increase patient satisfaction — a win for everyone.

With some adjustments, doctors can still make meaningful connections with patients, even within the constraints of modern healthcare. Renewing focus on compassionate, patient-centered care is the key. The doctor–patient relationship is a powerful therapeutic tool that we must not neglect. As doctors, we have an ethical duty to engage with patients in a compassionate and dedicated manner. Taking time to truly understand patients' perspectives and concerns, while explaining diagnoses and treatments clearly, is essential.

Another thing that can help is the use of software in your routine outpatient practice. At our hospital, we use software for outpatient records, which helps to keep the information organised and provide them with clean prescriptions. Even if the patient visits after a long time, say two years, we can always refer their previous records and remind them of the previous visit. This level of communication immediately builds trust and confidence, showing that the doctor is knowledgeable and considerate enough to help him get better. It's funny how often we hear, 'Dr. Atin, we know you will be having our record'.

How do you connect with patients on a personal level?

As doctors, we have a unique opportunity and responsibility to forge meaningful relationships with our patients. Our time with them is often brief but incredibly impactful.

Did you know that the average doctor in India spends only 2–5 minutes face-to-face with any patient?

That's just a startling fact for those of us in the medical profession. Our careers are built around helping people, yet we have so little time for meaningful interactions.

This is a challenge we can all relate to. Our days are filled with quick consultations, rushing between appointments, and piles of paperwork. It's easy to feel disconnected from the service that called us to this field.

But every interaction is an opportunity. What if we approached each brief encounter with fresh eyes and an open heart? How much could we achieve with focused presence and compassionate listening?

Even a short visit allows us to see the person behind the symptoms. Simple acts of warmth and understanding can uplift someone's day. When we give our full attention, those few minutes can hold profound meaning.

Another example is of a teenage patient, which I'll never forget. He was struggling with depression but reluctant was to talk about it. One day, I noticed he was wearing a T-shirt from a band I liked. I complimented his shirt, and we ended up chatting about music for a bit. That simple connection opened the floodgates. It was the breakthrough that allowed him to start opening up about what he was going through.

My point is: never underestimate the power of human connection in healthcare. Small gestures and conversations can make a huge difference in how comfortable patients feel with us. When we relate to them as people first, the medicine follows more smoothly. Taking time to truly see our patients is worth it and they deserves nothing less. Communicating with the patients during rounds, with their kids nearby also build trust, establishing humanism.

Connecting with patients on a human level allows me to truly understand their needs and provide the best care. There's nothing more gratifying than seeing a patient improve under my care. Their smiles and thanks make all the long hours worthwhile.

However, patient interaction can also be emotionally draining. When treatments aren't working or diagnoses are bleak, sharing difficult news with compassion takes an emotional toll. I've shed tears with more families than I can count. Without rich patient interaction, I wouldn't be the doctor I am today.

As a doctor, the most rewarding part of my job is interacting with patients. I'll never forget the first time I diagnosed a little boy with asthma. Seeing his eyes light up when he could finally breathe easily after treatment was a magical moment.

My patients give me purpose and drive. Their openness motivates me to keep learning and improving. I'm a better doctor because of what I learn from every patient. At the end of the day, it's all about the connections. That's what makes this profession so meaningful.

Let's renew our dedication to truly seeing our patients. We have the power to heal hearts as well as bodies.

Being a doctor isn't just about diagnosing diseases and prescribing medications. The most fulfilling part of practicing medicine is developing meaningful relationships with patients.

While knowledge and technical skills are crucial in medicine, never underestimate the healing power of a warm smile, a reassuring hand squeeze, and taking the time to listen. My patients have taught me so much over the years. I'm thankful for the privilege of walking with them on their healthcare journeys and making a difference through a caring human connection. This is the art of medicine.

How do you make meaningful connections with patients in your practice? I'd love to hear your thoughts and experiences!

At your next appointment, try having a real conversation and listening attentively. Learn what matters most to that person sitting across from you. Build trust and rapport through genuine interest in their life outside your office. You'll be amazed at how little things like remembering a patient's favorite sports team or asking about their kids can transform their healthcare experience.

How do you prioritize connecting with patients amidst the demands of modern healthcare? I'd love to hear your insights!

Write down to me what you feel @ My contact details: authordratin@gmail.com or Whatsapp me @ 9888079179

10

THE IMPORTANCE OF TEAMWORK IN HEALTHCARE

We've all heard the saying "it takes a village." This is especially true in medicine. Life as a doctor can be isolating. Long hours in the clinic or hospital often mean you're on your own for most of the day. It's easy to feel disconnected from colleagues and team members. But we all know that medicine works best when it's collaborative. As doctors, we don't work alone — we rely on an entire team to deliver the best possible care to our patients. Teamwork is essential in healthcare, especially for doctors. Working together leads to better patient outcomes. Patients benefit from a team approach where various specialists weigh in. And for doctors, sharing the load reduces burnout and boosts job satisfaction.

As doctors, we don't just take care of patients - we take care of each other too.

That's why I'm fascinated by the impact of collaboration in healthcare. Studies show that effective teamwork between doctors, nurses, and other providers leads to better patient outcomes. So how can we foster this kind of collaboration?

It starts with communication. Making sure everyone is on the same page about the patient's condition and plan of care is critical. At Indrani Multi-speciality Hospital, a NABH accredited, with a motto of 'caring for life', situated in the heart of city, we begin each shift with a quick huddle to get aligned. We also do bedside shift reports so the oncoming nurse can meet the patient.

We also leverage each other's strengths. A good team recognizes that different people bring different skills to the table. I lean on our pharmacists' expertise in medications, especially Ravi Goyal, who is an expert in his field and managed to get the life-saving medications like 'REMDESEVIR', during toughest time of Covid era. Our physical therapists' knowledge of mobility, and our social workers', Nilesh Pethani, Pankaj Bhardwaj excel in coordinating patients discharge plans and well-being.

I'll never forget the time my team saved a patient's life. The young patient came in with multiple complex issues. No doctor could figure it out alone. But together, we pieced together the clues. I suggested a diagnosis, the cardiologist proposed another, the neurologist added a third piece. Finally it clicked -- the patient had a rare autoimmune condition. Because we worked together, we were able to start the right treatment immediately and the patient later made a full recovery. This not only helped the patient but also enhanced our hospital reputation. That case showed me the power of teamwork in medicine. No single doctor has all the answers. But when we collaborate, we can solve even the most difficult medical puzzles.

Most importantly, we have each other's backs. In tense situations like codes, we trust each other to do their jobs. This trust was evident, when a short circuit in the autoclave room triggered the fire sensors. Our in-house rescue team acted immediately, dispersing the situation and ensuring everybody's safety. Being a multi-speciality hospital, several issues arise every day. I recall a technical glitch causing the lift to get stuck. Our rescue team approached the site, rescued the people in the lift, ensured their safety. Teamwork in a hospital extend beyond treating patient, involves handling emergencies with a sense of responsibility.

Healthcare teams are like sports teams. We each have our positions and plays. But the magic happens when we work in synchronisation towards a shared goal.

The bottom line is that teamwork saves lives in medicine. But collaboration doesn't happen by accident : it takes intention, communication, and mutual support. When we work together, we can achieve so much more than the sum of our individual contributions. Our patients deserve nothing less.

Team Collaboration: The Lifeblood of Doctors

As a doctor, you know that medicine is not a one-person job. Caring for patients requires constant collaboration between nurses, specialists, technicians, and more. But teamwork doesn't always come naturally, especially in high-stress environments like hospitals. As doctors, we often focus on diagnosing and treating patients. However, providing quality healthcare requires collaboration within a team. During my morning rounds, I usually brief my staff with, 'No doctor can do it all alone'.

Have you ever wondered how doctors work together as a team to provide the best possible care for their patients? Collaboration is essential in healthcare, yet it can be challenging when each doctor has their own expertise and perspective. So how do they do it?

Unlike most professions, a doctor's work directly impacts human lives. They carry an immense responsibility that requires coordination across specialties to diagnose, treat, and care for patients.

Effective collaboration enables doctors to leverage each other's knowledge and skills. By communicating openly, understanding roles, and resolving conflicts, a healthcare team can deliver coordinated care. For example, a primary care physician may consult specialists to create a comprehensive treatment plan. Nurses closely monitor patients and provide updates on planned-out decisions.

I witnessed seamless teamwork first-hand when my grandmother was hospitalized. Her complex condition required input from cardiologists, nephrologists, and internists. Daily rounds brought together residents, nurses, and therapists to assess her progress. They discussed adjustments to her care plan and coordinated their efforts. Thanks to their collaboration, my grandmother made a full recovery.

Poor communication and lack of role clarity can undermine team collaboration. Without it, patient care is compromised. Medical errors increase, diagnoses get delayed, and frustration mounts between colleagues. But strong teamwork has the opposite effect. It fosters efficient care, creative problem-solving, and mutual support. So, how do we get there?

Throughout my career, I've seen how team collaboration improves patient outcomes. Make team collaboration a priority, not an afterthought. Set expectations for cooperation, define roles clearly, and create spaces for team huddles and debriefs. Seek input from every team member and value their perspectives. When disagreements occur, mediate compassionately. And appreciate your teammates often – collaboration thrives on mutual trust and respect. With intention and effort, your team's synergy can transform patient care. Collaboration allows us to provide a well-rounded treatment by combining our expertise.

I remember the COVID era, where everybody was frightened not to treat the patients, creating a barrier. On the other side, the team at Indrani Hospital was the talk of the town. We cared for patients by providing the best possible nursing care, medical facilities while displaying awareness protocol for patients/relatives , distributing free mask, ensuring hand hygiene by following all the Covid protocols laid down by the government from time to time.

To all doctors out there, I encourage you to actively participate in collaborative care. Seek input from your team, provide feedback, and keep communication open. We all have the same goal of helping our patients. By working together, we can achieve more. Make collaboration a priority in your practice for better patient care.

The key is recognizing collaboration as the lifeblood of medicine. Make it a habit, not a luxury. Your patients, and your colleagues, will thank you.

A recent study found that miscommunication was a factor in 30% of all indemnity claims and nearly 70% of medical errors. These shocking statistics highlight a major problem in healthcare — lack of team collaboration. As doctors, we all strive for the best patient outcomes. But the hard truth is that we are only human. Fatigue, stress, and communication breakdowns can all contribute to mistakes.

This is where team collaboration comes in. Research shows that effective collaboration between doctors, nurses, and other providers can reduce medical errors by over 30%. When we function as a cohesive unit, we each bring our own unique skills and perspectives. Together we fill in the gaps that any one of us may miss individually.

So, how do we build that teamwork? It starts with mutual understanding and respect for each member's role. Open communication allows us to speak up when we spot potential problems. And a shared dedication to patients' wellbeing unites us.

Effective communication and coordination between doctors, nurses, specialists, and other medical staff isn't just ideal — it's absolutely essential. Lives depend on it. That's why building a collaborative team environment needs to be a top priority in every hospital and medical practice.

So, how can healthcare organizations foster true team collaboration for doctors? It starts with leadership setting the tone and prioritizing a team mentality. Create spaces and times for doctors to connect, share knowledge, and align on patient care plans. Recognize doctors who engage in collaborative practices. And use technology platforms that allow seamless coordination across roles. With the right culture and tools, doctors can work closely together to provide the best possible patient-centred care.

While the healthcare field still has a long way to go, there are promising signs. More facilities are prioritizing team-building initiatives and cross-training to break down silos. And new technology is making it easier to share patient data and coordinate care plans across departments.

The takeaway is clear — improving collaboration pays off. It leads to fewer errors, better care, and most importantly, saves lives. When doctors, nurses and other staff function as a true team, 'the real winners are the patients.'

The key is moving from isolated doctors to a connected team. When physicians collaborate, patients win and this is the concept set by the hospital, under my leadership, providing services in medicine, critical care, orthopaedics, urology, dialysis, blood bank, general surgery along with diagnostic facilities including blood testing, X-ray, ECG, TMT all under one roof. By supporting one another, we can provide the safest, highest quality care. Our patients' lives are in our hands — together, let's do right by them. 'When we collaborate, we all win'.

How has being part of an amazing healthcare team made your job more rewarding? Please share your stories below!

This chapter is for all the doctors, nurses, and medical professionals who want to spread the word about the importance of teamwork in delivering great patient care. When we work together, we can achieve more. How have you seen collaboration make a difference in patient care? I'd love to hear your stories!

Write down to me what you feel @ My contact details: authordratin@gmail.com or Whatsapp me @ 9888079179

11

EXPLORING SPIRITUALITY IN THE MEDICAL FIELD

Do you feel like your work as a doctor lacks deeper meaning? Have you lost your passion for healing others? This is for you.

Being a doctor is an immense responsibility. Many doctors feel like they have lost their sense of purpose in their work. As a doctor, you hold lives in your hands every day. Have you ever wondered about the deeper meaning and purpose behind your work as a doctor? In our busy modern lives, it's easy to get caught up in the day-to-day demands of medicine and lose sight of the bigger picture.

Medicine is a spiritual calling, reflecting on the spiritual aspects of being a healer can be incredibly rewarding. Reconnecting with your purpose can reinvigorate your practice. Spiritual practices like meditation, prayer and journaling can help you tap into your deeper motivations. Taking time to quiet your mind, opens up the guidance within.

Reflecting on why you became a healer allows you to re-centre your intentions. Doing this even for a few minutes a day can dramatically shift your perspective.

I have been working as an intensivist for the past 20 years. As a doctor, I often deal with life-or-death situations. The immense responsibility can feel overwhelming. The hours are long, the work is draining, and there's little room for anything outside of medicine. Like many doctors, I found myself fully focusing on my career, neglecting other aspects of life.

Over time, I realized I needed more balance. I began exploring spirituality and finding ways to nourish my soul. Now I start my day with meditation, creating space for stillness and reflection. I recite prayers asking for guidance before big surgeries. I've joined a community of healthcare professionals who share spiritual resources. On my days off, I spend time in nature, go to religious services, or do yoga activities that remind me there's more to life than work.

My faith in "Balaji" grounds my work. "When patients are facing life-threatening illnesses, they often grapple with existential questions. My faith helps me connect with them on a deeper level. I've prayed with patients, provided spiritual counselling"

Dr. Deepali, an oncopathologist, finds solace in daily meditation. "As a doctor, I see intense human suffering. Meditating keeps I centred so I can be fully present with patients during their hour of need and provide them with the correct diagnosis"

For doctors like us, spirituality and medicine go hand in hand. This shows how faith and contemplative practices allow physicians to provide care with wisdom, empathy and integrity.

Pursuing spirituality has made me more grounded, compassionate doctor. I'm better able to be fully present with patients and their families during difficult times. I have a deeper sense of purpose in my healing work. While medicine is still demanding, I now have outlets to process the intense emotions that come with this job. My spiritual practices sustain me so I can continue caring for others. For doctors seeking more meaning, know that you don't have to do this work alone. Spirituality can be an incredible source of support.

Cultivating spiritual practices is a common solution that more doctors should consider for routine day-to-day stresses. Whether it's prayer, meditation, finding community at a place of worship, or exploring nature, spirituality can help renew meaning and restore purpose. Connecting to something larger than oneself — be it God, nature, or humanity — provides perspective. It's a reminder that every day as a doctor is an opportunity to alleviate suffering and make a difference. For doctors who feel disenchanted, incorporating spirituality into their lives may help them rediscover the profound privilege of their healing vocation.

The intersection of spirituality and medicine is complex. But these doctors reveal how spiritual grounding equips them to handle the joys and challenges of healing. The medical field needs its talented doctors to thrive, not just survive. By nourishing the soul as well as the mind and body, spirituality can sustain doctors through the intense demands of this essential work.

Spirituality in medicine is about connecting to something larger than you. It's about finding meaning in your vocation beyond just diagnosing and treating illness. Spirituality may mean different things to different doctors -- for some it's a religious faith; for others, it's a general sense of awe at the human condition. But essentially, it's what grounds you and reminds you of the sacred trust and responsibility you have as a physician.

If you feel your spiritual well running dry, make an effort to refill it. Try taking a mindfulness meditation course, going on spiritual retreats, joining a community of like-minded colleagues, or just spending more time in nature. When your inner life is rich, your ability to heal others will also flourish. Consider how nurturing your spiritual side can positively impact your practice and your patients. In our rushed, technology-driven world, maintaining your sense of meaning and purpose as a doctor has never been more important. Attending to your spirituality is essential for professional longevity and truly fulfilling your calling as a healer.

How do you maintain your spirituality as a doctor? This is a question many physicians grapple with.

However, spirituality is a unique aspect of the human experience and an important part of overall wellbeing. Let me explain.

Studies show that doctors who actively cultivate their spirituality are less susceptible to burnout. They report higher job satisfaction, more compassion for patients, and an overall greater sense of meaning and purpose. Spirituality provides inner resources to handle the intense pressures of the job. It offers a framework for processing the complex emotional responses that arise in practicing medicine. In essence, spirituality allows doctors to be more fully human.

Let me tell you a story about myself. I pray or meditate before seeing patients each morning. This centres and reminds me of my intention to treat humanity in each person. I also sets aside time on my days off for spiritual practices that replenish me — going to temple, gurudwaras, journaling, being in nature. While I sometimes struggles to make space for these habits, I find it's essential self-care enables me to show up as a best self for patients.

This reminds me, when I feel exhausted, I often move to Salasar Balaji Mandir, Rajasthan. My family and I start every year with a visit to Salasar Balaji Dham for his blessings, keeping him motivated, full of positive energy.

Another spiritual calling occurred when I visited Haridwar with my friends. The contentment felt after bathing in the Ganges was beyond comparison. Being a religious person, I also visited Dwarkadhish (Gujrat), Badrinath, and Kedarnath to get the divine blessings.

A doctor's job is to heal, and true healing encompasses more than just the physical. Doctors see people at their most vulnerable -- when they are sick, suffering, afraid. In these moments, compassion and humanity are as crucial as medical expertise. A doctor with a rich inner life, a sense of meaning and purpose, can provide care that nourishes the soul as well as the body.

Doctors who cultivate their own spirituality have higher job satisfaction, less burnout, and stronger connections with patients. Reflecting on life's deeper questions helps doctors cope with the stress of their work and renew their sense of vocation. Spiritual practices like meditation and prayer support doctors' wellbeing and resilience.

Doctors don't need to be religious to be spiritual. An appreciation for life's mysteries, a moral compass, a sense of awe at the human condition -- these spiritual sensibilities allow doctors to see their patients as a complete person and approach their work with wisdom, empathy and grace. The most skilled diagnostician may miss the mark without an open heart.

Spirituality also relates to feeling content. It is not about worshiping holy places but also helping others which are purpose of your life. Treating the poor gives you feeling of contentment. Donating blood to save life of someone's life is a spiritual act. I have donated blood 25 times and feel contented in doing such activities that save life.

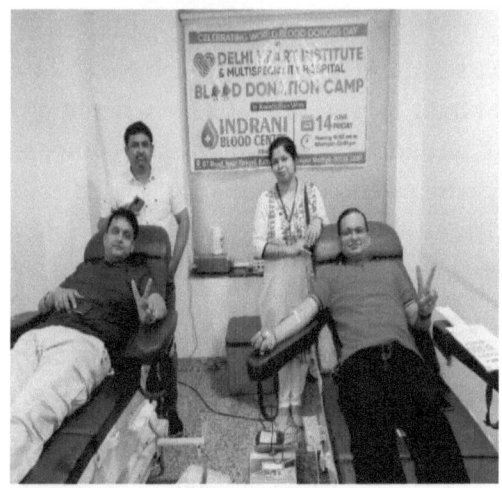

In the end, nurturing one's spirituality makes for more holistic, compassionate, and resilient doctors. For physicians, exploring this dimension of life can be incredibly enriching both personally and professionally. The demands of medicine make it easy to neglect, but perhaps this question deserves more attention.

In the intense world of modern medicine, nurturing one's inner life may seem like a luxury. But spirituality is a vital resource for doctors seeking to provide care that truly heals. The work of healing extends from the body into the soul. A doctor's spiritual life is not just a private matter - it ripples outwards into every patient encounter.

A recent study found that over 75% of doctors say that spirituality is an important part of their lives. This startling fact shows that spirituality still matters to the people responsible for saving lives every day.

As a doctor, you know how emotionally and mentally draining your job can be. Long hours, life-or-death decisions, and the immense responsibility you carry can weigh heavily on your mind. This is why spirituality offers an oasis of calm and meaning. Whether it's through prayer, meditation, or simply feeling connected to something larger than yourself, spirituality helps renew your spirit so you can continue to care for others.

Some doctors even report that their spiritual practices make them more compassionate physicians. Spirituality reminds them of the preciousness of life and provides inner strength during times of turmoil. It gives hope when medical options run out and brings equanimity when faced with the ups and downs of the job.

So don't be afraid to nurture your spiritual side. It's an invaluable resource for maintaining your mental health and becoming the best doctor you can be. Patients need your expertise, but they also need your empathy. Spirituality allows you to connect with your patients on a deeper human level -- which is the heart of great medicine.

Don't wait until you're burned out. Start today. Set a reminder to pause and meditate for 5 minutes. Journal at the end of your shift about moments that filled you with purpose. Share insights with colleagues to support each other. Discover the spiritual side of medicine again. You'll be amazed at the transformation.

What are your thoughts? I'd love to hear how you keep your spiritual flame alive in your medical practice.

How does your spirituality shape your approach to your profession?

This chapter is for medical professionals and others interested in the role of spirituality in demanding careers.

Let me know if you need anything else!

Write down to me what your take on spirituality @ My contact details: authordratin@gmail.com or Whatsapp me @ 9888079179

12

LEGACY BEYOND THE WHITE COAT

The concept of "Legacy beyond the White Coat" is a powerful theme, that encompasses the immense impact and contributions of medical professionals beyond their immediate roles in healthcare. This highlights the broader influence that doctors, nurses, and other medical practitioners can have on society, culture, education, policy, and community well-being.

1. Medical Professionals as Educators

Imagine the quiet moments in a bustling hospital where a seasoned doctor takes a young intern under their wing, sharing not just the intricacies of medical knowledge, but the wisdom of years spent in service. These mentors shape the future of medicine, instilling values of compassion, resilience, and unwavering dedication. Their legacy is not just in the lives they save, but in the countless lives touched by those they teach. This is exemplified by the dedicated guidance of Our boss, Dr. Jayshree Ghanekar, senior doctors like, Dr. Abhijeet, Dr. Harsh, Dr. Atul who have mentored many, among my colleagues namely Dr. Raman, Dr. Shital, Dr. Vijay, and Dr. Saket.

- Public Health Education: Initiatives to educate the public about health, wellness, and disease prevention in the form of free medical check-up camps, awareness camps, blood donation camps.

2. Innovation and Research

In the solitude of a research lab, late into the night, a scientist works tirelessly, driven by the hope of a breakthrough that could change the world. Each discovery, each innovation, is a beacon of hope for patients and families desperate for answers. The legacy here is one of relentless pursuit of knowledge and the courage to venture into the unknown, knowing that the fruits of this labor could save millions. Doctors contribute in Medical Scientific Research that advances medical knowledge and treatments. Innovations like robotic surgery, advanced medical software (complying with NMC guidelines), and the integration of AI in healthcare highlight the power of research and technology in medicine.

3. Advocacy and Policy

Picture the determined face of a physician standing before a government panel, passionately advocating for healthcare reform. Their voice carries the weight of countless stories of patients denied care, of communities in despair. Through their efforts, policies are shaped, systems transformed, and lives improved. Their legacy is a testament to the power of advocacy and the profound changes that can be achieved through perseverance and justice.

- Healthcare Policy: Involvement in shaping healthcare policies and advocating for healthcare reform.

- Public Health Advocacy: Working towards policies that improve public health and access to healthcare.

4. Community Engagement and Service

Visualize a rural community clinic where a (Auxiliary Nurse and Midwife) ANM nurse spends her weekends providing free medical services. She knows the names and stories of every patient, offering not just medical care but hope and human connection. The legacy here is one of deep, unwavering commitment to community, of being a lifeline for those often forgotten by the broader healthcare system.

- Volunteer Work: Participation in medical missions, free clinics, and community health fairs.

- Leadership in Non-profits: Leading or supporting organizations focused on health-related causes.

5. Humanitarian Efforts

In the heart of a crisis, amidst chaos and suffering, stands a doctor, delivering care in the most challenging conditions. Their presence brings solace and healing, a reminder of humanity's capacity for compassion even in the darkest times. This legacy is etched in the grateful eyes of those they help, a beacon of hope and humanity's resilience.

- Global Health Initiatives: Efforts to combat diseases and improve health outcomes in underserved regions by educating people about eye and blood donation and realizing the importance of the same.

- Disaster Relief: Providing medical care in the aftermath of natural disasters and humanitarian crises like COVID. Doctors, nurses along with paramedical staff were the first to get vaccinated to assure safety for all.

6. Ethics and Compassion in Medicine

Consider the quiet, powerful moment when a doctor chooses to sit with a dying patient, holding their hand, offering comfort in their final moments. It's in these moments of profound empathy and respect for human dignity that the true spirit of medicine shines. The legacy is one of ethical integrity, compassion, and the recognition of every patient's inherent worth.

- Patient Advocacy: Ensuring patients receive fair and compassionate care.

- Ethical Medical Practice: Upholding high ethical standards in medical practice and research.

7. Cultural Contributions

Envision a physician-author whose words bridge the gap between the medical world and the public, offering insights and stories that illuminate the human condition. Their books inspire, educate, and comfort, becoming a source of strength for readers worldwide. This legacy is one of storytelling that heals, educates, and connects us all.

- Medical Professionals as Authors: Writing books, articles, and memoirs that offer insights into the medical profession and its impact on society.

- Media Presence: Participation in media to spread awareness about medical issues and influence public opinion.

8. Personal Stories and Biographies

Imagine reading the memoir of a medical pioneer whose journey was filled with challenges and triumphs. Their story becomes a source of inspiration, a testament to the human spirit's capacity to overcome adversity and make a lasting impact. This legacy lives on in the hearts of those inspired to follow in their footsteps.

- Inspiring Journeys: Sharing personal stories of medical professionals who have made significant contributions beyond their clinical duties.

- Legacies of Medical Pioneers: Highlighting historical figures in medicine whose work has had a lasting impact.

9. Interdisciplinary Collaboration

Picture a bustling conference room where doctors, engineers, social scientists, and artists come together to solve a pressing health issue. This collaboration leads to ground-breaking solutions, born from the blending of diverse perspectives and expertise. The legacy here is one of innovation through unity, proving that together, we can achieve the extraordinary.

- Cross-Disciplinary Work: Collaboration between medical professionals and experts in other fields such as engineering, social sciences, and the arts to address complex health challenges.

10. Sustainability and Environmental Health

Visualize a green hospital, where every effort is made to reduce environmental impact. Here, doctors and administrators work together to promote practices that protect both human health and the planet. This legacy is one of foresight and responsibility, ensuring a healthier future for generations to come.

- Environmental Health Initiatives: Efforts to address the environmental determinants of health and promote sustainable practices within healthcare settings.

Potential Formats and Activities

- Conferences and Seminars: Hosting events that focus on the broader impact of medical professionals.

- Publications: Producing articles, books, or documentaries that explore these themes.

- Awards and Recognition: Creating awards to honor medical professionals who have made significant contributions beyond their clinical roles.

- Workshops and Training: Offering programs to help medical professionals expand their expertise in these areas.

Exploring "Legacy beyond the White Coat" can provide a comprehensive understanding of the multifaceted roles that medical professionals play in society and highlight their contributions to the greater good beyond direct patient care. Their contributions extend far beyond their clinical duties, touching lives, shaping futures, and creating a legacy of compassion, innovation, and unwavering dedication to the betterment of humanity. Their stories inspire us to see the world not just as it is, but as it could be, through the lens of tireless effort, boundless empathy, and an enduring commitment to making a difference.

Let's delve deeper into each of these areas with a more emotional and evocative tone, capturing the essence of the profound impact medical professionals have beyond their immediate duties.

Thank You.........

FINAL THOUGHTS

As I reach the end of this journey, I find myself reflecting on the themes and ideas that have shaped this book. Writing it has been an exploration of not only the topics discussed but also of my own experiences and beliefs. Each chapter is a reflection of the lessons I've learned, the challenges I've faced, and the victories that have shaped my path.

This book is more than just a collection of thoughts; it is a piece of my soul, a window into the passions that drive me as a doctor, entrepreneur, and community leader. My hope is that the insights shared within these pages will resonate with you, inspire you, and perhaps even challenge you to think differently about your own journey.

To my readers, thank you for allowing me to share this part of my life with you. Your engagement with these ideas is what gives them meaning. It has been an honor to write this book, and I hope it serves as a valuable companion on your path to growth and understanding.

As you close this book, I encourage you to continue exploring, questioning, and striving for the best version of yourself. The journey is ongoing, and the possibilities are endless.

With sincere appreciation,

Dr. Atin Gupta

Author I Life Saver I Enterpreneur

www.ingramcontent.com/pod-product-compliance
Lightning Source LLC
LaVergne TN
LVHW041850070526
838199LV00045BB/1528